LAW AND OUTLAW

Also by William Vance

DRIFTER'S GOLD
DEATH STALKS THE CHEYENNE TRAIL

LAW AND OUTLAW

WILLIAM E. VANCE

DOUBLEDAY & COMPANY, INC.
GARDEN CITY, NEW YORK
1982

Library of Congress Cataloging in Publication Data

Vance, William E.
Law and outlaw.

(A Double D western)
I. Title.
PS3572.A425L3   813'.54
ISBN: 0-385-17460-8   AACR2
Library of Congress Catalog Card Number 81-43374
Copyright © 1982 by William E. Vance
All rights reserved
Printed in the United States of America
First Edition

LAW AND OUTLAW

CHAPTER 1

He came on the bloodied land when the sun was not yet up. Only two months out of Tucson, Will Titus did not come looking for gold, land, furs or peace. He was there, in Utah Territory, in the heart of Mormon country to take an outlaw.

He'd spent a week in the hills around Circle City keeping out of sight. It was easy to do in that savage land of up and down mountains, enormous arid valleys, scraggly brush, tortured trails and men on the run. Moving by night, he watched from cover by day. With the long glass he spied on the town he'd grown up in, watching the town he'd grown to hate.

At last, satisfied with what he'd learned, he headed toward Circle City in the dark hours before morning, planning his entry into the town as carefully as a General Grant campaign.

A pink glow in the sky above the black, jagged outline of the mountain on the far side of the valley hinted of the coming sun as he rode out of the twisting canyon, suddenly widening into the flat country surrounding Circle City. He had circled from the south so as to enter the town from the north. He was a careful man in all respects.

Nearness to the town of his boyhood brought an unfamiliar ache within his chest. He put down an urge to hurry. He reminded himself of the emigrant train somewhere between St. Joe and this lonely savage valley in which the entire train had been attacked by saintly Mormons dressed as Indians. All but a few of the hundred and twenty-five emigrants, men, women and children were cold-bloodedly slain.

He was one of the survivors.

U.S. Marshal Will Titus was well-mounted on a black gelding of sixteen hands. He rode warily with a watchful, roving eye on his surrounds, a dim trail winding among stunted oak, sagebrush and thistle. He had a lined, somewhat broad, expressionless face, with a black mustache trimmed to the corners of his thin lips. His skin, exposed to the weather, seemed like very old leather.

He appeared to be a whole, competent man but actually he was crippled in his right hand. Only Titus and his Tucson doctor knew that his widely known and unbelievable skill with a Colt Peacemaker had been destroyed by the slash of a drunken miner's knife, cutting the tendons of his right wrist.

He had not let this handicap deter him in his job as U.S. Marshal, Arizona Territory, though he was troubled at times that someone might discover his secret and take advantage of the fact that his skill with a gun was no longer what it once had been. He had gained a certain secret facility with a .38 Smith and Wesson that he carried tucked under his right arm in a spring clip holster.

He rarely worried about things he could do nothing about.

An almost unseen movement of the scrub oak ahead caused him automatically to drop across the neck of his horse. He muttered a curse as his right hand habitually reached for the Colt .45 on his right thigh; then his left hand swept to the .38 as a yellow flash lighted the area. Leaning forward, he fired to the right and below the flash of gunpowder.

Titus knew his single bullet had struck flesh. He knew it from the sound. He knew it from the feeling of the gun in his hand. He had experienced all of this in his time.

There was a thrashing sound in the underbrush, a sound that slowly diminished and suddenly stopped. An owl hooted somewhere in the early dawn and a late-flying bat swooped down and flashed away. In the far distance he could hear faintly a howling dog, a mournful sound.

The black horse stood quite still as he'd been trained to do. Titus dismounted, dropped the reins to the ground and walked slowly ahead, his pistol held loosely in his right hand, though he'd fired it with his left.

He stepped cautiously around the head-high brush oak and stared down at the man sprawled motionless on the ground, face down. The man lay on the stock of a long-barreled single-shot Sharps rifle. A hunting knife was sticking in the ground beside the body. Titus grunted. He thought: that was to finish me off if he didn't kill me with the only bullet he had in his rifle.

As he stood there the man moved and murmured fitfully. Hastily transferring the .38 to his left hand, Titus knelt beside the man and rolled him over with his knee, shivering as with a cold wind blowing down his neck as he did so.

"God damn it to hell," he muttered aloud.

This man on the ground was not a grown man but a smooth-faced boy whose eyes opened wide at that moment.

"Why'd you try to bushwhack me?" Titus asked harshly, trying without success to overcome his remorse.

"Why—I—I reckon I'm a friend of—" and his voice trailed off without finishing and Titus knew he was dead.

Titus squatted a moment, looking down at the fair face now fully revealed in the gray dawn; thin, colorless hair on his upper lip, tangled light brown hair. A battered round-crowned black hat lay beside the knife.

How had this boy known where to wait for him, Titus wondered. An expert at detecting men who followed him for various reasons, mostly those wanting to kill him, Titus had not spotted this young one. Was he, Titus, getting careless or old or losing his touch?

"God damn it to hell," he muttered again and stood upright.

He replaced the .38 in the spring clip holster under his right arm. Slowly he drew the black-handled .45 from the worn holster on his right thigh and thumbed back the hammer. He fired a round into the ground, wincing at the wrist pain of his effort. He ejected the spent shell from the .45, making certain

it fell on the dead boy. He inserted a fresh round from his car-
tridge belt and holstered the pistol.

The spent brass shell, lying on the dark clothing of the boy,
glinted like a gold nugget in black sand.

Titus turned and walked slowly to his horse. Standing there
beside the patient animal, he stroked its neck. He glanced at
his back trail. Nothing there. He saw nothing, heard nothing
but the rustle of the scrub oak under the light wind, the stamp
of his horse and soft chime of the bit chain.

Stepping away from the horse, he surveyed the country on
all sides. The sky was a lighter pink in the east and a few elon-
gated clouds topped the mountains.

He was not a man easily worried but for the first time in his
career as a lawman he'd been stalked without knowing it.

His thoughts reached back to where he was yesterday, hidden and secure in a small valley above the town. He'd seen distant riders from time to time, unobserved by them because he
was well hidden. He'd seen nothing suspicious then or since.
Yet he'd been ambushed. Not a man alive should have known
when and where he'd planned to enter Circle City.

CHAPTER 2

The candle on the bedside table laid a weak, flickering yellow light in a small irregular circle. Elizabeth Laney took a last look at her sleeping mother before pinching out the candle. She walked through the dark silent house to let herself out through the front door.

She had a deep and firm conviction that her brother Bart had returned to the country of his boyhood.

She stood on the top step for a moment, adjusting the gray shawl over her head and around her shoulders. In the months that had passed since she knew Will Titus was returning to Circle City, she'd been depressed, excited, nervous and calm in unpredictable spells.

Her mother lay dying, in a drugged sleep. Her brother Bart had sworn to see her before she died. Bart was one of the most-wanted outlaws in the country. Will Titus was one of the most skillful manhunters in the country.

It wasn't nearly full light when she stepped in easy strides through the dark and sleeping town. There was a reddish quarter moon over the dark mass of mountain to the east.

Her heartbeat quickened with expectation. Why had she suddenly decided that Bart was here—or near? She'd *felt* his presence.

She was thirty-eight years old that spring and many years past what the locals called an old maid. She thought of herself differently. She'd had many a proposal and she'd turned them all down. She wondered how much Will Titus had had to do with all those decisions, some of them high pressure, such as that from the leading churchman, Bishop Adam Cantrell.

She turned in at the temple which was half-completed now, tripping over a block of stone in the darkness. There was a light on in the sheep wagon and even though the canvas cover was darkened with age and weather, she could see the dim outline of Dave Grubbs, the stonemason.

She tapped on the door and heard Grubbs walk across the wagon. The door opened. He was too tall to stand erect in the sheep wagon so he squatted in the opening, shaking his head from side to side at the question in her eyes.

"No, ma'am, he ain't here yet." Grubbs was a brown-faced, brown-eyed man with curly black hair and a full beard. He was a Gentile. There were no Mormon stonemasons in the entire county. Bishop Cantrell had brought Grubbs from Salt Lake to built the temple with the help of volunteers.

She knew that Grubbs had lived for a time in Bishop Cantrell's stone house nearby but when there was talk of Grubbs and Elvira, Cantrell's widowed daughter, the sheep wagon had been brought in from the range and made available for the stonemason's use.

He smiled at Elizabeth, a sudden showing of white teeth that she found attractive. "He'll show up one of these days," he observed reassuringly.

"I hope it's not too late," she said.

"I'll bet your ma will hang on 'til he gets here," he said, his manner somewhat hesitant, recognizing the delicacy of his remark.

Elizabeth wasn't worried about her mother living until Bart got there. She wanted Bart to get there before Will Titus did. But she didn't explain to Grubbs.

She stepped off the stone block that served as a step and turned away. "Let me know the minute he gets here," she said and stepped with that same long stride toward her home.

It had been arranged with all the lookouts surrounding the town that Bart would be directed to the sheep wagon when he finally arrived in the area.

Dave Grubbs stared hungrily after her for a moment, naked lust in his brown eyes. Then he slammed the door shut and

surveyed the tiny enclosure that on the range normally served
a sheepherder as living quarters. There was a narrow bunk, a
tiny stove that somehow reminded him of a pregnant woman
and a shelf that held his provisions. There was a ten gallon keg
of water that he filled from Cantrell's well every other day.

Bishop Adam Cantrell barred Elizabeth's way when she was
abreast of his house, an imposing structure built of the same
stone that was being quarried to construct the temple.

A huge man, Cantrell was more than six and a half feet tall,
with wide, powerful shoulders and without an ounce of fat. He
held himself stiffly erect at all times with his majestic head
held high. His silver-streaked beard was always neatly
trimmed and combed. She wondered which of his six wives at-
tended to that chore.

Cantrell dressed conservatively well as befitted the religious
and civil leader of all the people in that part of the Territory;
except, of course, the Gentile community a few miles south of
the Troublesome River, made up of non-believers who had, in
a moment of hilarity, named their town Gentility.

"You shouldn't be trippin' around all hours, Elizabeth," he
said in his gentle yet somehow severe voice.

"I had to know."

"Don't you trust me—us?"

"Of course I do. Maybe I'm too impatient."

"I also am impatient," he said, "for another reason."

She flushed and did not answer.

"Have you thought about what you'll do when Martha is
gone from us?"

My mother, she thought, is still some protection to me.

"No," she answered.

"Then you'd better give it serious thought. You're a beautiful woman, Elizabeth, but you're nearing forty. You should
bear children to comply with God's Commandments as revealed to the Prophet Brigham, bless him."

She thought: my god, Brigham's been dead ten years and
Adam still invokes his name. "Yes, sir," she said dutifully, in-
tending to give it not another thought.

Cantrell gestured toward his house. "This home awaits you."
"You built it for—"

His raised hand and fierce look stopped her. "I built it for
whomever God and I want there." He stared at her, his fierce
look fading as quickly as it appeared. "Go home. You'll know
when the time comes. You'll know when Bart gets here, I
promise." He wheeled, strode across the ground and disappeared into the stone house.

She stood there irresolutely for a moment, then firmly turned
and stepped, slowly now, toward the sheep wagon. She forced
herself to walk up to the closed door, where she tapped, now
timidly.

The door opened at once. Grubbs stood there, frowning,
staring down at her in puzzlement.

She said, "That look on your face, in your eyes, when you
look at me. It doesn't offend me."

His mouth opened and he stared at her.

She put her foot on the stone block and stepped up into the
sheep wagon. It smelled of stale food, sweat, bacon and the
sharp odor of cement.

She began removing her shawl when two shots sounded dis-
tantly, and their movements froze.

Grubbs broke the silence. "Get out," he said in a hoarse
whisper, his face twisted with fright. "All I need is for Bart to
find me and you—"

Titus mounted the black and rode toward town, balancing
the Sharps across his saddle. Later, he stopped, staring at a
gate that had been constructed in his youth, across the road
leading into Circle City. Rulers had mandated a gate at either
end of town with twofold purpose: to keep range cattle out of
the town proper and to collect toll from strangers passing
through Circle City. The gate was abandoned when ranchers
moved their cattle to more distant range; and when strangers
found they were expected to pay a toll, they simply went
around the town.

"Get, Peso," he spoke to the black and went on.

A new stone temple was being built north of the ward house. Walls of stone were rising. A wide, flatbed wagon, still loaded, stood before the temple where the driver had left it. Titus remembered the area on the mountain from which the vividly colored stone had been quarried.

He stopped his horse with a slight pressure on the reins. A sheep wagon, its wheels removed, rested on four stone blocks, placed under the axles. The canvas-covered wagon stood close beside the unfinished temple. As Titus watched, a tall bearded man stepped down from the wagon and stared at him. He stood there, motionless, a dishpan in both hands. He tipped the pan and tossed the water out and without speaking, turned and reentered the wagon.

Titus rode on. A horse and buggy stood before Doc McNair's frame house. The horse, an ancient, bony roan, stood hipshot, head down. Doc slumped in the seat, head lolling, his boots jammed against the mudguard.

The black stopped of its own accord, beside the buggy. Titus looked down at McNair who snored softly, his mouth open, his black bag on the seat beside him.

Titus thought: god, he looks old. He looked at McNair's old familiar residence, a combination office and living space. It wasn't much: A square, two-story frame, almost exactly like the undertaking parlor next door; beyond the undertaker's was the dusty cemetery, enclosed with a three-strand barbwire fence.

McNair's house, unpainted, uncared for, like the man who owned it, held a weathered sign beside the front door:

P. McNAIR, M.D. & VET
TEETH PULLED
HERBS THAT HEAL
INVIGORATING TONIC

and in very small print:

minor surgery

Titus smiled. The tonic was McNair's personal concoction, made of mineral oil, herbs and a generous portion of alcohol that McNair manufactured in one of his upstairs rooms.

Doctors, as were lawyers, were viewed with dark suspicion by the Mormons, a view vigorously promoted by all church presidents starting with Brigham Young.

In fact, in earlier times, McNair had almost starved to death for lack of business, before he branched out. There were some who said he paid too much attention to womenfolk.

Titus remembered him as a dark, slim and handsome man when McNair arrived quietly in Circle City and set up practice. Now his black hair was generously streaked with gray. His face was wrinkled and he needed a shave. His waist was no longer slim; there was more than the beginning of a paunch.

McNair stirred as Titus looked down at him thoughtfully. Doc straightened, rubbing his eyes with both hands and then looking at Titus. He looked all around as though to discover his whereabouts.

"Well, by gum, ol' Nellie got me home again. Just so tired I couldn't get outta the buggy." He looked more closely at Titus and exclaimed: "Will Titus, by god!" He straightened and held out his hand.

The two men shook hands.

"I'm surprised you remember me."

McNair chuckled. "Good lord, how could I forget? You and Bart—why I sewed up and fixed up you two more than any dozen kids in town." His face grew serious. "We heard about your coming. We're all troubled. Everybody, even the bishop."

Titus was silent for a time while the black stamped restlessly and swung his head down to gnaw a fetlock. "How is Mrs. Laney?" Titus asked.

"Sounds strange hearing you call her Mrs. Laney."

"She's not my mother."

"She treated you like a son. Some say better'n Bart, even."

"I always wondered why Matthew gave me my own name,"

Titus said. "He didn't have to do it, you know. And I'd have never known."

"Matthew had principles."

"I suppose so."

"You should forget all those old wounds, Will. It's not natural. You didn't know any of those people who were killed. Not even your own father and mother."

"My uncle took care of that," Titus said dryly.

"You asked about Martha. She's dying. She'll go any day now. I see her a couple of times a week but only to make sure she has pain killer."

"Elizabeth?"

"Still unmarried," McNair said shortly. "Shameful waste. She spends her days—and nights—taking care of her mother. She has no other life." He got down from the buggy, stiffly, rubbing his back. "I'm going to put Nellie away and try to get some sleep. People around here never call on me 'til it's too late. Good day to you, Will." He took Nellie's bridle and began leading the horse around the house toward the small barn and corral.

"Doc."

McNair stopped and turned to face Titus.

"Doc, I killed a boy early this morning. He tried to ambush me. Had an old .50 caliber buffalo gun."

McNair was silent for so long Titus spoke again: "If I'd known he had a single shot rifle, if I'd known he was a wet-eared kid, it might have been different. I didn't know."

"Will, Will," McNair said in a despairing voice. "That boy would be George Fenton. Bart Laney was his hero. He always had visions of joining Bart. I imagine he thought killing you would make him eligible."

"Maybe it would."

McNair didn't answer but led his horse around the house and out of sight.

Circle City had not changed much, Titus mused, as the black walked quietly through the sleeping town. There was a coolness in the air that would last until the sun was two hours above the mountains. He saw a woman moving along the edge of the road ahead.

For a moment it seemed his heart stopped. And then raced madly. He quickened the pace of the black with a word.

Elizabeth stepped faster at the sound of his horse.

He turned the horse across the road and came up behind her as she reached the Laney home, with its neat white picket fence bordered inside by flower beds, colorful, and perfuming the air.

She glanced quickly over her shoulder, smiled uncertainly and then stopped, turning slowly, not looking at him.

"Elizabeth," he said quietly.

She tilted her face to him, meeting his cold blue eyes with her smoky gray ones, with a hint of defiance.

"We've expected you," she said. "Ever since—"

He tipped his hat back to reveal a contrasting band of white between his shock of black hair and sunburned bronze face.

"How's Mrs.—how's your mother?"

She tilted her head in a way he remembered and the shawl dropped to her shoulders, showing the pale gold hair above a high forehead. She had the same thin, sensitive nostrils of her brother Bart, he noted for the thousandth time.

"What you really want to know is, is Bart here?" Her nostrils flared and her eyes sparkled. "No, Will, no. He won't come."

He leaned forward, crossing his hands on the saddle horn and kicking his boots loose from the stirrups, sitting loosely in the saddle, a big, compact, competent-appearing man with a touch of ice in his pale blue eyes. "You didn't answer my question, Elizabeth," he said quietly.

"Please, Will," she said in almost a whisper and turned away from him.

He didn't move, not revealing the heavy thump of his heart. Her voice reminded him of when he was twelve, holding a bird he'd caught in his hand, feeling the hurried beat of the tiny heart. Elizabeth had been with him then, crying out for him to release the bird.

"She's not any better, Will. She'll never be any better." She came around slowly, her eyes down, not looking at him. "Bart won't come back, Will. He knows that you, or the Pinkertons, or somebody will be waiting for him. Why don't you go back, Will? Let others to the dirty work."

"I have my orders."

"From whom? The railroad? The bankers' association? The cattle kings?"

"I'm a United States marshal. A President appointed me."

"You're called the mankiller marshal."

"Any man I've gone after has had a choice," Titus said. "He could come along peaceably or fight. It was always his choice, not mine."

"There's none I know could stand up to you."

"None you know," Titus repeated reflectively.

She blushed. "None I've heard about."

The black stamped impatiently and switched his tail. Titus put the toe of his expensive boots into the stirrups and lifted the reins. "I want to see your ma," he said.

"She's asleep now, Will. But when she wakes up you can see her." She opened the cover of a small watch on a chain around her neck. "The pain killer will be wearing off in an hour or so. I'll send word. Where are you staying?"

"I haven't found a place. Where would you recommend?"

She stared at him. "There's not a boarding house, not a hotel, not a home in Circle City'll take you in, Will."

"Old Grafton still live across the street?" He tilted his head toward the house directly across the road from the Laney home.

She nodded. She closed her eyes and lowered her head, snapping the watch cover shut again. She turned and went slowly to the gate and pushed it open and walked the flower-bordered walk to the front porch. She turned there and looked at him wordlessly.

"I'll be waiting at Grafton's store."

She didn't reply but crossed the porch, opened the door and entered without another glance at him.

He felt a strange sense of defeat, something that was new to him.

He thought: I'm not going to let it get to me. I'm going to handle it just like I'd handle any other job, any other time, any other place.

He didn't convince himself in the least.

He sat there for a moment longer, feeling the rays of the now-warm sun, wondering why the town slept so late. He spoke to the black and let the horse walk up the road to Grafton's General Store, just beyond the blacksmith shop, where he dismounted and tied in at the warped, cracked rail.

Standing there, he took another look around before climbing the steps to the store; it was closed. A man came out of the boot and saddle shop next door and began sweeping the porch, raising clouds of dust.

The porch of Grafton's General Store ran the full width of the false-front building. Across the street was the small county courthouse, built of the same quarry stone as Cantrell's house, the same stone being used to build the new church.

Peering through one of the dusty windows, he could see the glass case near the center of the main entrance, where Grafton kept alive the false legend of the Circle Valley Massacre. He stepped back and looked over the assortment of seats. He could take the long bench against the wall, a broken-armed rocking chair, or a chair made from a barrel with a rawhide seat. He chose the broken-armed rocker and sat in it, waiting for the town to wake up.

The man next door finished sweeping and went back into the leather shop. Down the street, across from the Laney house, a tall, thin man emerged, tugged at his vest and turned resolutely toward Titus. Elmer Grafton, the storekeeper.

While he waited for Grafton, Titus thought: it's not a job I want but I can't help myself. All the U.S. marshals stationed in

Utah Territory were chasing polygamists. Washington had ordered him out of Tucson to intercept Bart Laney if and when the outlaw visited his dying mother. Washington did not know that he, Will Titus and Bart Laney had been closer than most brothers at one time. Or did Washington know?

Elmer Grafton mounted the steps on stiff legs and stopped before the double doors of his store. He half-turned to face Titus.

"Marshal Titus, I believe?" he said in a raspy voice.

"Yes, sir. Where is everybody?"

"Our citizens are filled with awe and fear. They come out only when they have to. You're bad for business, Marshal." He watched for Titus' reaction to this judgmental statement and heartened by none he could detect added: "The most famous marshal looking for the most famous outlaw."

"Bull," said Titus.

The storekeeper colored and coughed. "It's in all the papers," he blurted. "Even the ones back east. All the bounty hunters, all the mankillers and shooters, all the undesirable element in the west are converging on Circle City at this very moment. Even the great Mark Twain is rumored to be on his way here to interview you."

"All wanting a front seat at the meeting, eh?"

Grafton nodded.

Titus looked up and down the street. "You still a bachelor, Mr. Grafton?"

Grafton stiffened and then his head jerked up and down. "Why, yes, I am, if it's any of your business."

"It is." Titus' voice was hard and cold. "Keep this to yourself. I've reason to believe I'd have trouble finding a place to live while I'm waiting for Bart Laney. I don't want to be put to the trouble of finding out. I want to camp on your front porch while I'm here. I'll pay you well and be no trouble to you."

Grafton swallowed rapidly, his Adam's apple bobbing up and down. "How—for how long?"

"Maybe a day, maybe a week or a month. However long it takes."

"I'm a very private person, Marshal," Grafton said in a weak voice. "I'd have to think about it. I'd have to discuss it with Bishop Cantrell."

"Think it over," Titus said, "but don't talk to Cantrell about it."

"I—I'm one of his counselors—"

"I don't care if you're his adopted son," Titus said curtly. "Don't discuss it with the bishop."

"If you feel that way," Grafton said, "all right."

Titus nodded and massaged his right wrist with his left hand.

Grafton took a big iron key from his coat pocket and looked at it as though seeing it for the first time. He unsteadily inserted it in the lock and turned it. Before opening the door he said, "Marshal, I've a housekeeper. Her name is Jenny Gardner. She'll tend to your needs."

"I'll tend to my own needs."

Grafton opened the door to his store, stooped to unlatch the second door and swung them both wide. He disappeared into the interior.

The familiar smell of Grafton's store floated out to Will Titus, bringing back more unwanted memories. He resisted the urge to get up, walk into the store and look at the little museum Grafton had created to the memory of Matthew Laney, Bart's father. Titus knew it all without looking. The campaign hat with the faded yellow cord. The tarnished sword. One glove. And the document:

March 23, 1877—Captain Matthew Laney was executed at Sunrise today, for the alleged murder of 120 Gentile men, women and children, all members of a California-bound wagon train. The execution, on the site of the so-called Circle Valley Massacre of more than 20 years ago, was carried out by Deputy U.S.

Marshals as none of the faithful could be found who would agree to do the dastardly deed, executing an innocent man.

Captain Laney refused a blindfold and sat calmly on his coffin box awaiting his death as he had lived out his exemplary life, courageous, unflinching and with faith intact in God, Church and Family.

He is survived by the widow, Martha, and daughter, Elizabeth, both at home in Circle City, and a son, Bartholomew whose whereabouts is not known.

Titus put it all out of his mind. He thought: it's all a goddamn lie, every bit of it. I don't give a tinker's damn if the truth never comes out.

He knew he lied to himself.

CHAPTER 3

"I'm Town Constable Thomas P. Riley. These two are my sons, Ephraim and Moroni."

Riley was short, broad-shouldered, a dark-bearded man with an air of dread on his rough face. One of his sons, Moroni, was an exact replica of Thomas P. Riley; the other, Ephraim, was tall, sandy-haired, bucktoothed, with a vacant expression on his slack face and a matching look in his deepset hazel eyes.

"How do," Titus said, nodding at each one in turn.

"You're Marshal Will Titus, I take it?"

"Yes."

Riley braced himself visibly. "I saw a picture of you and Bartholomew in Miz Laney's parlor. You look different."

"I'm older," Titus said.

Riley's voice was apologetic. "I have to ask you about young Fenton, George Fenton. There was an empty shell casing on top of his body. I've heard that that is your mark."

"I'm sorry about young Fenton," Will Titus said emptily. "He tried to kill me from ambush."

"I sort o' suspected that," Riley said resignedly.

Will Titus thought: if I'd known he was a kid. If I'd known he had a single shot rifle. If, if, if. "I suppose Fenton has a whole passel of vengeful kin?"

Riley shook his head. His two sons shook their heads. "No, he was an orphan. Both his parents died in the Indian uprising six years ago. Bishop Cantrell let him sleep in the barn and do odd jobs."

"Then what do you want of me, Constable?"

"The impossible, I reckon. I'd thank God if you'd leave here and never come back."

"That's impossible, all right. I have my work cut out for me here."

"Our women are afraid to venture outside. Our children are even worse off. Some little girls hide under the beds."

"They've nothing to fear from me."

"I believe you. But the others who are here because of you . . ." Riley's sons again nodded affirmation.

"I've seen no others you speak about," Titus said.

"They're all around, camping here and there, waiting for Bartholomew, just as you are." He raised his eyes piously to the sky. "They are out there, Marshal, more the pity."

"You seem to be an honest man. You are a fellow officer of the law, sworn to uphold the law—"

Riley put out his two hands and violently protested almost unintelligibly. He regained his speech and said, "Don't put me in the same class you're in. I've been constable ten years and never made an arrest. I pick up strays and serve papers and things like that."

"As I was sayin'," Titus went on as though Riley had not interrupted, "it may be that some of these fellers riding in here are wanted men. I'm familiar with most of the wanted ones. If I know them and I see them, then, naturally I'll take them into custody."

"Circle City has no jail."

"I have ways," Titus said evenly.

"That means you'll kill instead of arresting?"

"That's usually up to the man I'm after."

Elmer Grafton appeared in the doorway of his store. He wore a clean white apron that reached to his ankles. He had black sleeve holders just above his elbows. A round-eyed boy of about sixteen peered around his arm.

"This is Jason Gardner, Jenny Gardner's only son. He helps me around the store."

"He looks like a good hard worker."

"Jason's a good boy, Marshal. And it's a shame. He saw you sitting here and was afraid to pass you. He come around to the back door and knocked to be let in."

"Now that is a shame," Will Titus said. When he rose to his feet, Jason's face showed alarm and he ducked back into the store.

"Come out here, Jason," Titus called. "You just been introduced to me proper and I want to shake your hand."

Jason came timidly from the store and walked closer to Titus and hesitantly held out his hand which shook visibly.

Titus took Jason's hand and shook it briefly.

"There now, that didn't hurt, did it?"

Jason shook his head dumbly. "By George, gee, I just shook hands with Marshal Will Titus," he said disbelievingly.

"For what it's worth."

"Worth aplenty to me. I bet there ain't a man in the whole Territory wouldn't give a lot to do what I just done. Is it true that you shot it out with three top guns down Arizona way and got 'em all?"

"More or less," Titus said dryly. "Now, why don't you get on with your work?"

"Yes, sir!" He reached inside the door and brought out a straw broom and began vigorously sweeping the porch, raising a cloud of dust, all the while casting quick glances at Titus as Titus slowly rocked and watched the Laney house.

The broom slowed, then stopped. "I guess I ought to tell you," Jason said haltingly.

Titus' gaze swung around and he eyed Jason. "Tell me what?"

"Fenton. George Fenton. I knew he was gonna do it."

"Do what?"

"Try to kill you. He told me he was going to do it. He told me how, too."

"Why didn't you tip me off?"

"I didn't even know what you looked like. Except that picture in Miz Laney's parlor. That one of you and Bart."

Titus made an encouraging sound.

"Anyway, George wanted to be like Bart. He was always ridin' up to the roost country where Bart got started."

Titus nodded, remembering, and murmured, "Yes, where Bart got started."

"Me, now, I wanted to be like you, Marshal. Law and order an' all that." He stood there, leaning on the broom, his eyes wide. "Maybe I could help you, could I, Marshal?"

"You might be able to help me," Will Titus said judiciously. "I got to sleep some time. I can't watch day and night."

Elmer Grafton came through the door and spoke crossly to Jason: "Get on with it, boy."

Jason jerked erect, said, "Yes, sir!" and disappeared into the store.

Grafton cleared his throat noisily. "Marshal, looks like I'm not going to get any business long as you sit here. So I'll put you up at my home while you're in town."

"That's mighty decent of you, Mr. Grafton," Titus said, rising. "I'll just walk my horse down to your barn, if that's all right with you."

"Turn him in with my buggy mare," Grafton said without enthusiasm. "I just hope he don't teach her how to jump the fence."

"Not a fence jumper."

"Glad to hear that. My housekeeper, Jenny Gardner usually comes about now. Just tell her you'll be staying for a spell." He moved back into the store, muttering to himself.

Disdaining the steps, Titus jumped to the ground. He untied his horse and walked toward Grafton's neat frame house across the road from the Laney residence.

He stopped. The blacksmith shop stood back from the road about sixty feet, sheltered by a giant cottonwood tree. He remembered it, the blacksmith shop, as Milo Shapp's barn long, long ago. Titus and Bart and Elizabeth had played in the dim interior, hiding in the hay, jumping down from the loft into high piled grass hay, or swinging on the rope used to haul hay up to the loft from wagons on the ground. The sign over the shop simply said: LUCIAN BOWMAN, SMITH.

Lucian glanced up from his labor as Titus wrapped the reins around a snubbing post near the shop. A tall, bulky man, his fiercely red hair and beard were sprinkled with white. He had been working on a coffin stretched between two sawhorses, a box of white pine stroked into satiny smoothness.

"I heard you was in town," Lucian said, resuming his rubbing of the coffin.

"Mighty nice looking coffin," Titus offered.

"Nothin's too good for Martha Laney," Lucian said and paused, glancing at Titus from small, deepset green eyes. "You should know that, Marshal, better'n anybody."

"I do."

"Then act like it and get out of the country."

"I got a job to do," Titus said patiently, "and I'm bound to do it."

"If God is willing, you mean."

"Well, yes, He might have something to do with it."

"You better be almighty certain He has something to do with it. My son Brace wants to talk to you."

"I'm willing to talk to anybody about anything."

"There's no warrant out for Brace. Him and Bart alluz been good friends, that's all."

"I know of no warrant for Brace. What's he up to?"

"He wants to make a deal for Bart."

"Well, now, that's mighty interesting." He thought: Brace Bowman, Bart's sidekick since maybe '77 or thereabouts, noted for sartorial splendor, even on the run. Never connected with any robbings, shootups or anything to do with the old Robber's Roost gang; but involved, nonetheless. Brace had a legendary skill with a hand gun almost equal to that of Laney—or me.

"As I remember, Brace has red hair, too."

"You remember well. He comes by it rightly enough."

"When will the coffin be ready?"

Lucian shot a penetrating look at Titus. "It's been done, boy," he said. "I'm just givin' it an extra lick or two. Nothin' much else to do."

"When do you reckon she'll be needing it?"

Lucian gave him a hard look. "You're different, Will. Seems when you and Bart were runnin' around, a couple of wild kids, you were somewhat alike. Maybe you're no different now?"

"What I don't need today is a sermon," Titus said with a trace of irritability.

Lucian ignored his irritation. "And then there's you and Elizabeth. Everybody knows how you felt about her. How can you take the only brother she's got left, maybe kill him?"

"Bart went one way, I went another. Look, you see anything different around town, let me know."

"Lord help us, everything is different in this town."

"You know what I mean. I'll be staying over there on Grafton's front porch."

"You'll be lucky not to catch a bullet sitting there in broad daylight. Will, what you're askin' is for me to tell you if and when Bart is around. I like you, Will, alluz thought you a good boy. But I can't do what you want and that's a simple fact." He bent back to his task of improving on perfection; Titus felt he was being dismissed.

He untied the gelding from the snubbing post and led him to Grafton's front porch, where he off-saddled. He stacked his saddle under the window. He carefully moved the rocking chair away from the window and placed it halfway between the front door and the window. He shoved the chair against the wall and then pulled it forward far enough so that when he rocked the back of the chair wouldn't strike the wall. He stood his sawed-off 12-gauge Greener, Winchester and Fenton's Sharps against the wall beside the rocking chair. He picked up his valise and led the black around the back of the house to Grafton's small corral and buggy shed.

Grafton's bay mare was in season, rubbing her backsides

against a fence post. The black arched his neck, pricked up his ears and prancing, whickered softly.

"Your memories ain't gonna do you much good," Titus sympathized, as he stripped the bridle off and tapped the black into the corral.

He hung the bridle on the gate post, picked up his valise and strode toward the creek, just beyond the corral. It was shadowed there, from the cottonwoods and willows that grew close to the water.

There was a slight curve in the creek with the shallows on this side. The water seemed to be deep on the far side. He stood there for a minute or two, looking the area over. Satisfied, he hung both hand gun rigs on a limb projecting over the water. He stripped down to bare skin and hung his clothing on the willows. He found his bull bladder bag of soap in the valise, scooped out a handful and waded out into the creek.

He washed all over, including his hair. Afterward he floated in the deep part of the pool, looking up at the sky through the leaves of the trees.

Afterward, he shaved, trimming his mustache carefully and using the tip end of the razor to get the hair growing from his nose. He splashed water on his face and dried with his dirty shirt. He took clean clothing from his valise and dressed. He pulled on his boots last and used the shirt to remove any vestige of dust from them. He pulled his pants legs down over the boots, stowed everything and went back to sit in the rocking chair on Grafton's front porch.

He had exchanged the dark clothing he wore into town for a fawn gray coat, vest and matching pants. He pinned on his badge as he sat there, feeling a twinge in his right wrist.

From where he sat he had an unobstructed view of the Laney house and the area all around it, except directly behind the house. Anyone approaching from the back would have to come across an open space unless they could get as close to the ground as a snake. He felt reasonably satisfied.

CHAPTER 4

His name was Shagrun and he'd killed a man in Amarillo for jostling his arm when he was taking a drink in the Oasis Saloon.

He got out of town in a hurry because the dead man was popular locally; and an observer had exclaimed, "Sheriff Meaney catches you, he'll shove his gun up your ass and empty it!"

The entire countryside knew that Sheriff Meaney was well-named.

Shagrun fled.

He'd been on his way to Circle Valley anyway, and he saw no reason to dillydally along the way, especially in Amarillo.

Nearing noon he sighted the smoke of a campfire two miles below Grafton's (or was it Cantrell's?) grist mill on the Troublesome River, some two miles west of the cluster of saloons, brothels and gambling houses called Gentility.

Shagrun was still raging from having to run for it. He'd killed once before, shot a man in the back on a dark night, but he felt he had the makings of a, say, Ben Thompson, Clay Allison, Wes Hardin, and some of those other killing sonofabitches.

He could handle just about anything, he reflected, as he headed for the smoke. He could sense that in this country of orderly homes in town, the well-organized community life of a Mormon town, that the smoke came from outsiders.

He wasn't wrong. Not a man squatted or sat around the smoldering campfire. He sat there for a minute, enjoying himself, and then called: "Come on out, it's me, Gil Shagrun."

Three of them emerged slowly, their hands resting on or near their pistols.

Shagrun recognized one of them. "Hi, ya, Milt," he said.

Milt Pelkey, unshaven, unwashed, with grease and dirt encrusted trail clothing, and wearing a pair of shotgun chaps, nodded and spat a stream of yellow juice and didn't bother to wipe his chin.

"Hi, ya, Shagrun," he said, and came to squat before the fire. "Come up for the hullabaloo?"

Shagrun nodded and dismounted as the others resumed their places around the fire. He joined the circle next to Pelkey.

"We wuz too, 'til we found out Titus is here."

Shagrun's eyes narrowed and then brightened. "Marshal Will Titus? Yeah, that why I'm here," he lied.

"We kind of lost interest when we heard about Titus. He ain't no man to dick around with." He squinted at Shagrun. "You come on accounta Will Titus?"

"Yeah, I figger to get some tiger meat."

Milt Pelkey uttered a raucous bray. "Hey, lis'n to that! This pilgrim done gone batty. He's gonna take on Titus!"

The other two eyed him owlishly.

Milt continued, "I knowed you a long time, Shagrun. I alluz thought you had more sense. Hell, you couldn't stand up ag'in Will Titus anymore'n I could throw my hoss across the Troublesome."

"You're a talky sonofabitch," Shagrun said and pulled his pistol and shoved it in Milt Pelkey's face, a sudden blind rage contorting his face and walling his eyes. "Open yore mouth, little man, and suck on the end o' my ol' .45."

Milt grinned weakly. "Aw, shoot, Shagrun, I wuz—"

"Go on, open yore damn mouth. That's the way it is most o' the time anyhow." He thumbed back the hammer of the Colt.

Milt opened his mouth and Shagrun placed the gun barrel between Pelkey's yellow snaggleteeth. After a tense moment he pulled the gun out of Pelkey's mouth and fired over his head. Pelkey scuttled off into the brush.

Shagrun blew in the barrel of his gun and leisurely rose to his feet and moved toward his horse, still holding his gun. He mounted and rode up the river, the other two men watching him.

One of them looked at the other and shrugged. "Craziest goddamn bunch of people in the world out here," he remarked.

"Damn if I don't believe you're right," the other agreed. "That crazy bastard's gonna go up there and get his ass shot off."

A man in homespun came out of the grist mill as Shagrun reached the wooden bridge spanning the Troublesome. He stood there impassively watching Shagrun who had halted his horse in the middle of the bridge.

"Where'll I find Marshal Titus?" Shagrun asked.

The man was silent for a moment and then he spoke: "Second house on the left straight ahead. You're comin' into Circle City."

Shagrun nodded, raised his hand, rode on. He'd visualized facing Titus and felt confident in his speed and skill with a gun. He'd done a lot of practicing drawing and dry firing. He couldn't afford shells.

That state of affairs wouldn't last long now. Doing in Will Titus would make a big man of him overnight. He could have his pick of any law job in the country. It was said that a county sheriff made plenty of money and maybe he'd try for one of those. With the fame that came to a man who beat Will Titus there'd be no trouble at all.

He thought: I've heard that feller Behan down in Tombstone country makes forty thousand a year sheriffing, collecting taxes and fines and such. That oughta be a good place to start. Behan could just have an accident an' make it all the easier.

He stopped his horse in front of Grafton's house and looked at the man in the rocking chair on the front porch. He thought: he don't look like much of a much.

He stepped down from his horse on the off side and tested drawing his pistol half out of the holster just to make sure it wouldn't hang up. He walked around his horse and strode to the gate and stood there.

Titus had lifted himself from the chair and was leaning the point of his shoulder negligently against a porch post. The thumb of his right hand was tucked into his belt and his left hand rested on the lapel of his gray coat. He seemed bigger than when he sat in the chair.

When Shagrun looked into Titus' eyes something made an icy impulse run up and down his spine.

"Marshal Titus?" His voice sounded uneven to him.

"The same," Titus said, sensing that this man had not stopped here to pass the time of day.

"What I come here to do," Shagrun said, his voice less ragged and stronger now, "is to find out if you are faster with a gun than me."

"There's no quicker way to hell," Titus said quietly, not moving at all. He thought: this crazy sonofabitch is going to draw on me. My hand couldn't get my .45 in a month of Sundays. I haven't developed any speed with my left, though if he hurries I'll have a chance.

Just a small chance.

Titus saw the sudden doubt that flickered in Shagrun's eyes. Titus moved slowly and deliberately away from the wooden post and descended the steps and walked forward until not more than six feet separated them.

A showdown at six feet takes more raw courage than at greater distances. Titus remained silent but alert, seemingly unconcerned and relaxed.

Sweat oozed from Shagrun's forehead. His lips twitched.

"Now what you're goin' to do," Titus said, "is turn around slow and face the other way. Unless you want a bellyful of lead."

There was something about Titus that seemed to overpower Shagrun.

Shagrun hesitated once, then turned slowly, jerkily, as directed.

Breathing easier, Titus stepped forward and lifted the pistol from Shagrun's holster. A dry sob escaped the man's throat.

"Get moving," Titus ordered, "head out for the blacksmith shop kitty-corner over there."

Lucian Bowman lifted himself from his labor on the coffin and turned as they approached.

"Lucian, this here thing that calls himself a man is wanted for murder in Arizona Territory. I'll take him with me when I leave. In the meantime, seeing as how Circle City has no jail, I want you to iron him up to your snubbing post."

"I ain't wanted for no murder," Shagrun whined.

"Shut up."

Lucian scratched his beard. "Who's gonna pay for it?"

"The United States government, of course. They always pay."

"Takes a mighty long time," Lucian grumbled. "Anyway, it ain't Christian to chain up a human bein' like that."

"I lay no claim to Christianity," Titus said. "Go ahead with it."

To Shagrun he said, "Sit on the ground there 'til he's ready for you. I'm going back to my rocking chair. I got a .44–40 Winchester right by my chair and I can knock the buttons off your shirt from Grafton's front porch. Only thing is I won't be shootin' at your buttons."

He wheeled to find that a small crowd had gathered. He looked at them stonily. "Go on about your business," he said and they silently melted away.

He walked slowly back to his post on Grafton's front porch, noting that Elizabeth's face was at the window with the curtain slightly parted.

As he resumed his seat, her face disappeared from view.

CHAPTER 5

Jenny Gardner bustled around the pleasant kitchen of her three-room cabin between the forks of the Troublesome River and Little Creek, the stream that meandered past Grafton's house.

She was perspiring slightly because the cook stove still threw off heat from the morning fire. Her upper lip was beaded with sweat. Her auburn hair, long and shiny-silk, was piled high on her head, the nape of her white neck exposed.

She pulled on her sunbonnet, tied the pink ribbons under her firm chin, preparing to walk to Grafton's store before going on to her work as housekeeper for Grafton, a job she'd held the seven years since her bill of divorcement was approved by Bishop Cantrell.

Jason burst through the kitchen door like a demented bull, his eyes alight with wild excitement.

"Guess what?"

"Why aren't you at work?"

She worried about Jason a good deal of late.

He ignored her question, expanding his chest and striding importantly up and down the room. "Marshal Will Titus is in town!"

"And who might be Will Titus?" she asked, closing the damper on the stove.

He scowled. "Don't you know nothin'? Titus is only the most famous marshal in the country. The fastest draw, the deadest shot. I bet he's killed a hundred men!"

"That's something to be proud of?" Without pausing, she

asked, "Why aren't you at work where you belong. Brother Grafton—"

"Hang ol' man Grafton," Jason said. "He makes me sick, so damn fussy, like an ol' woman—"

"Jason! Stop swearing! I mean what I say!"

"Oh, all right. But 'damn' ain't swearin'—"

"Don't sass me, young man! And you'll not quit your job." Red spots appeared on Jenny's cheeks, making her even prettier, her amber eyes blazing. "Now, back to the store with you —no, wait. Take Violet Cantrell's dress with you. She's to pick it up at the store today."

Jenny Gardner also did tailoring for some of the more affluent ladies of Circle City. None were more affluent than Cantrell's six wives.

"I won't do it," Jason said stubbornly. "Me, carryin' a dang dress." He suddenly grew excited again: "An' you know what else? Marshal Titus killed George Fenton this morning!" He thought: that'll fix her.

She stood quite still, suddenly dazed. "George Fenton? That boy you ran around with? Your best friend?" She went to Jason and put her arms around him. "It might have been you, Jason."

He wiggled out of her arms. "Who, me?" He laughed nervously. "Shoot, me and George weren't such good friends—"

She looked at him in bewilderment, at loss for words.

His chest swelled again. "George was alluz ridin' out to the Roost country. I might do that myself—if I had a horse."

"Why in the world would you do that?" she asked helplessly. "And we're not buying a horse."

"To give Marshal Titus a hand. I told him I'd help him out. He sort of halfway hinted I could do him some good."

"One minute you're going to help a law officer and the next you're going to be an outlaw," she said sarcastically. "Do wrong and you'll have your famous marshal after *you*."

"He's not here for but one thing," Jason said with great assurance, "an' that's to take Bart Laney when he shows up."

"Enough talking," Jenny said sharply. "Off with you."

He hesitated, rebellion rising, then grabbed the dress and stalked out, slamming the door hard.

"Handle that dress carefully," Jenny called.

Jason didn't hear, or elected not to answer.

Jenny went out the back door and looked at her vegetable garden and small orchard, noting that Jason had not done the weeding he'd promised to do. She took the back way to Grafton's store and did not see Titus on the front porch of Grafton's house.

She listened to Grafton's complaint about the influx of strangers in Circle City, to the poor quality of merchandise he had to pay top price for, the demands imposed on him by being a member of the bishopric and ended by informing her that Will Titus would be their guest for an indefinite period.

"But don't worry about him," Grafton cautioned. "He ain't going to be no trouble. He won't sleep in the house so you won't have another bed to make. He'll be bedding down on the front porch. Of my house!"

"He must be a strange man."

"Strange? Well, I don't know. He left here before you come so you wouldn't know about the other things."

"What other things?"

He waved his hand deprecatingly. "Better get over. He might be wanting something."

"I won't leave 'til you tell me."

Grafton gestured toward the glass case and miniature museum. "Titus was a member of the emigrant train, a boy when it happened. Laney raised him up to the time Matthew was indicted, tried and executed.

"Will's uncle, a blowhard Southerner from Arkansas come out and got Will and took him away. Poisoned his mind against the people who raised him." He busied himself rearranging a bolt of cloth. "I don't want to talk about it."

She recognized his limits. "That's plain to see," she said and walked out of the store.

Passing the smithy, she saw a man chained to Bowman's snubbing post. Lord deliver us, she thought.

She came into the yard of Grafton's house and stopped at the bottom step, looking at Titus. She thought: he's handsome but there's something forbidding about him.

He returned her look, guessing her age to be in the late thirties, observing her rather pretty face and her strong body with ample curves. Someone nice to snuggle up to on a cold winter night, he thought.

"You're Jenny?"

"Why is that man chained up over there?" There was a note of belligerence in her voice.

"Why, there's no other place for him. Circle City has no jail."

"I'm well aware of that," she said. "But to treat a human being like an animal—"

"He's worse than an animal," Titus said. "You wouldn't understand that kind of human critter."

"Maybe I would, maybe I wouldn't. Have you had anything to eat today?"

"I ate a bit of jerky a little before daylight," Titus said. "I'm not hungry right now."

"Men don't know the first thing about taking care of themselves," she said. "You're no exception, famous marshal or not. I'll bring you a glass of milk."

"Don't bother. I'm not going to cause anybody any trouble, that is not any more than I can help."

"Except the Laneys," she said. "I'm doing the wash today. You got any dirty clothes I can wash?" She looked distastefully at his saddle, saddlebags, valise, telescope, and array of guns, all stacked neatly against the wall beside the rocking chair.

"I cleaned up when I got here. There're a few dirty clothes in my valise."

She looked him up and down and despite herself found she was attracted to him. Somehow this irritated her. "Do you want to build a fire under my boiler pot in the backyard?"

"Sorry. I can't leave right now."

"Afraid Bart might slip in?"

"No. Elizabeth is going to call me when her mother wakes up. I want to see Martha."

"So does Bart."

"All he has to do is walk in and see her."

She bit her lower lip as she removed her bonnet. She let the bonnet dangle by the pink tie strings. "I hope you don't have too long a wait, Mr. Marshal."

"That's my hope, too. How long have you lived in Circle City."

"Seventeen years. Jason was born here."

"Jason's your son?"

She bit her lip again. "Yes. And don't be putting ideas into his head. I've enough trouble with him."

"Seems to be a fine young man."

"I think so but I'm his mother."

"Your husband—"

"I have no husband."

"What happened?"

"I don't know. Mr. Gardner went on a mission when Jason was a year old. I've not heard from him since."

Titus knew of the church system of sending men to do missionary work throughout the world. It was obligatory. He clucked sympathetically. "Think he'll ever come back?"

"I neither know nor care," she said stiffly. "I got a bill of divorcement seven years ago. Afterward I left the church."

"And they let you stay—"

"I do not wish to submit to your questioning," she said. She was angry, not with Titus but with herself because she'd allowed him to draw her out.

Without looking at him she lifted her skirt, stepped up to the porch and moved past him into the house without speaking.

He thought: she's quite a woman.

In a few minutes she reappeared with a bowl in her hand.

"Here's some oxtail soup left over from yesterday," she said. "You should have something solid inside you."

He looked at the bowl with steam rising from it and then looked at her. "Isn't that the stuff Brigham Young ate so he could keep all his wives happy and contented?"

She flushed. "I don't know that they were happy and contented. Do you want it or not?"

He accepted the bowl and balanced it on his knees. The smell was good. He stirred it with the spoon. "Why, I sure do thank you, Jenny Gardner. You're not only a pretty woman but you've a heart of gold."

Smiling, she felt a moment of pleasure at praise from this man, so different from men she'd previously met. Then she frowned. Why should she feel so gratified at a pat on the head from him? Who did he think he was?

"You probably haven't seen many women lately," she said tartly. "And knowing what my heart is like on such short acquaintance is presumptuous."

"Ah," he said appreciatively, tasting the soup. "The story I heard about this here oxtail soup, is that the servant who brought it every single day to ol' Brigham—"

"I don't want to hear it," she said, and fled into the house.

East of Circle City, rising out of the undulating plateaus, the La Sal and Henry mountain ranges provided sanctuary for the owlhooters, snakes, insects, Indians and whoever was on the run from whatever haunted their footsteps.

Spotted throughout the mountains were outlaw hideouts in what was called the Roost country. Robbers' Roost.

At one of these hideouts, a rough cabin in a secluded canyon, six men sat around a smoldering campfire outside the cabin, discussing the problem at hand: removal of Will Titus from the land of the living so that Bart Laney could visit his dying mother.

Five of the men looked at the man called Gorila, a bandito

with short legs, arms almost to his knees, a man with as un-
savory a reputation as could be found west of the Mississippi.
Chased out of Mexico by the rurales, he found a precarious ex-
istence stealing whatever wasn't nailed down, robbing country
storekeepers, ranchers, miners and occasionally being accepted
by the big time outlaws for a special job.

"It's a dead certain cinch," Ellie Bay stated, "that if we go
in together, Titus is gonna get at least three of us. Trouble is,
we don't know which three it would be."

All except Gorila nodded solemn agreement.

"Now, Gorila here, is the only one the marshal don't know
on sight."

"He is a dangerous man, señors," Gorila muttered.

"That's for dang sure. So we gotta trick him. He don't know
Gorila, like I said, so Gorila's the only one with a Chinaman's
chance to get close enough to him to kill him."

Gorila felt important. Here were some of the big ones accepting him. On the other hand their acceptance was based on
his killing the most dangerous man in the country. He tried to
put forth a semblance of an argument against his taking on
such a hazardous mission, one that would allow him to refuse
and yet remain within the inner circle.

His brain wasn't up to it.

An incredibly ugly man, his face had been caved in by the
kick of a mule at an early age. He tried to hide the damage
with a sweeping mustache; but that only accentuated his vil-
lainous cast. His wide shoulders and dangling arms made him
appear actually to be related to a gorilla, the source of his nick-
name.

"You ain't gonna be takin' much of a chance," Bay continued, not heeding Gorila's protest. "We'll get McNair to put a
splint on your right arm, to hide the gun. You'll just walk up
and let go. Titus won't suspect a man with a broken arm in a
splint."

"I ain't gonna do it," Gorila said.

Bay drew his pistol from his holster and cocked it. "I ain't inclined to argue a whole hell of a lot," he said. "But I'll blow a hole in your gut you can put your fist in if'n you don't do it."

Gorila shrugged. "Senor, where do I find this Doc McNair?"

Bay chuckled. "That's the stuff, Gorila. We knowed we could depend on you."

"We'll go with you to the doc," another added. "He might need some persuadin'."

A short plump man with bow legs and rounded shoulders raised his hat from above his eyes and cleared his throat. "Uh, Ellie, this is all good and alla that but Bart ain't gonna like it. I heard you promise him you'd not kill Titus—"

"I don't see no other way," Ellie Bay interrupted. A tall, slim and handsome man with blond hair and blue eyes, he was the outlaw generally recognized as Laney's closest friend and ally. He'd partnered Laney since the first major holdup, of a mining company payroll, elevating them to national attention with the size of the haul. "Bart won't like it but once it's done he'll see it's for the best."

"Don't say I didn't tell you."

Bay slapped the short man on his shoulder. "I'll sure remember that, Willie. Just put it outta your mind now and let's get Gorila down to Circle City." He looked around at the circle of faces, hard cases all. "You, Jack, take Ben and Sam. Don't ride through town. Circle around and come on Doc's place from out back. He'll be there or he'll be along directly. An' listen, don't hurt him too bad. Now get a move on."

He watched the four saddle up and ride out, staring moodily after them. He thought of Bart's resistance to killing Titus and he felt, as always, a twinge of jealousy at Laney's unfailing regard for Will Titus.

Other thoughts crowded in on Bay. He had a growing premonition that Laney was headed for his last days on earth. Will Titus was after him, close on his trail. That put a different cast on everything connected with this, what to him, was a foolhardy expedition. He had to think about what would happen to him and to the gang if Titus killed or captured Laney.

He stared speculatively at Willie as the small, round man puttered with the horses. That one was a troublemaker, and would be the first to go if he, Bay, had to take over the gang.

CHAPTER 6

Circle City hadn't been much of a town when he left it in his youth and it still wasn't much, Titus thought moodily, staring over the roof ridge of the Laney home to the dark reaches of the mountains beyond.

Clouds were building over those mountains. The wind drifted them like sailboats out over the valley. The sun made spotted, moving shadows on the valley floor.

From where he sat, in the rocking chair on the front porch of Grafton's house, Titus could see the tip of Cantrell's grist mill above the bridge over the Troublesome River. Without moving, except by turning his head, he could also see Grafton's General Store, the boot and saddle shop, and a small square unpretentious building labeled Cheese Factory. The road curved back toward the cemetery; he could not see Doc McNair's or the undertaking parlor on the opposite side of the street from Laney's house. He could not see the cemetery where Matthew Laney was buried, and where Martha would join him shortly.

A shock wave like a breath of wind and yet unlike a wind hit his face, bringing him alert and erect. He waited expectantly. A sullen boom of explosion reached his ears. The sound came from a distance, echoing and reechoing among the canyons.

He was pondering the cause of the explosion when Jenny Gardner came through the door, wiping her hands on her apron.

"Quarry blast," she said calmly, seeing the question on his face and his inquiring look. "They're getting stone for the church."

He settled back in the rocker.

"You'll get used to it," she said.

"How did you get here to Circle City?"

"I told you."

"I mean where did you meet him—Gardner?"

She thought: should I tell him the truth, that Arch Gardner came to San Francisco to meet a woman coming from England to be his bride? She wasn't on the ship and Gardner had to have another woman. He picked me from a whorehouse but I wouldn't have come if I'd known he had two other wives.

"I met him in San Francisco. He was there on business."

"I see."

No, she thought, you don't see. "I thought we'd settled the matter of discussing my life."

He stared at her for a moment and then looked away. She fled into the house.

Titus sat there for a long while, watching the clouds form over the mountain and float out over the valley. A creaking sound reached his ears. He heard the sound of a wagon crossing the bridge. A few minutes later the heads of oxen appeared around the curve in the road. Three yoke of oxen, pulling a heavily loaded flatbed wagon, stone blocks piled high, came into sight. The drover walked alongside the off wheeler. A yellow dog with a curled tail plodded along beneath the wagon. The freshly quarried stone, bright in the sun, streaked red and yellow in varied shades, was stacked neatly on the wagon bed and tied down with a clever arrangement of rawhide and wooden poles.

He watched with some interest as the oxen plodded past. The drover, as with other townspeople, did not look at him.

Gust Bogan was a manhunter by profession and by choice. He'd been a deputy sheriff in Colorado but had to run for it when he killed the husband of the woman he was seeing in secret.

The man he killed, a prominent townsman, made it impossible for him to continue in his capacity of deputy sheriff.

Bogan was one of those oddities of nature, a natural killer. He loved to kill. He'd killed men for as little as five dollars. He'd collected from rich cattlemen as much as five hundred for each killing in Wyoming.

When selling his services he'd tell a prospective buyer that he was the best. He'd tell them that no man was too tough for him to tackle. There had been several occasions where, when doubtful of the outcome, he'd shot men from behind, or laid in wait for them.

Along the rocky road of his life he'd picked up a partner for convenience sake. Now, the two of them were camped in a level piece of rocky ground below the crest of Paiute Point, just above the town of Circle City.

Bogan and his sidekick were there to collect the rich rewards offered by the Union Pacific Railroad, the Western Bankers' Association, the combined Wyoming and Montana Cattlemen's Association, and several other interested parties for the capture, dead or alive, of one Bartholomew Laney.

When the blasting in the rock quarry started, Bogan decided to not camp there, but to move on, away from the sound and activity.

Later in the morning the two of them found another and better campsite. It was at a lower altitude and afforded them a better view of the Laney home.

Bogan, the older, meaner and wiser of the two killers first spotted Titus.

Bogan, his spyglass in hand, stretched his massive form on the ground and rested the barrel of the telescope on a rock to steady it while he looked, one eye squinted shut, the other tight against the eyepiece.

"What is it, Gust, whatta ya see?"

"I ain't seen nothin' yet. Go get some firewood."

He moved the telescope from the Laney house to the man in the rocking chair on the front porch of Grafton's home. When he had satisfied himself as to the man's identity, he cursed roundly.

"What is it, Gust, what's it all about?" Manta Kile asked in his whiny voice.

Bogan sat up, wiping tobacco juice from his whiskered chin.

"Marshal Titus, that's what's the matter. Marshal Will Titus, by damn!"

Manta Kile blinked his small eyes rapidly. He was a wiry cowboy with limited intelligence. Bogan had picked him up in Montana because, he, Bogan, needed a camp flunky and a man who'd look up to him, obey unquestioningly. Manta Kile filled the order.

"Good god," Manta said, "let's get the hell outta here."

Bogan frowned at Manta and said nothing.

"Jeez, Gust, I—"

"Shut up!" Bogan roared. "I'm thinkin'."

"All right, Gust, all right. I jes'—"

"Goddamit, hush!"

Manta Kile fell silent, staring at Bogan as the big man slowly capped the telescope, placing it on his bedroll. He sat on the ground, his hands on his knees, staring down into the tree-lined road that meandered through Circle City.

"Bart Laney's head's worth ten thousand dollars, jes' from the railroad. An' about that much more from others, like banks and sich. An' I'm not goin' to cut and run jes' from Titus bein' here."

"What'll we do?" Manta asked in his whiny voice.

"We'll do what we gotta do. Kill that sonofabitch afore Bart gets here."

"Jeez, Gust, I don't wanna go up agin Titus."

"We'll watch him a spell," Gust said, speaking more to himself than to Kile. "Then we'll do some figgerin'."

The wind rose and rustled the brush. From where he sat Gust watched the road, brooding. He saw the wagon load of stone appear on the road from the canyon. His eyes narrowed as he watched the oxen plodding through town, raising a gray plume of dust.

Elizabeth came through the front door of the Laney home and beckoned to Will Titus.

He got leisurely to his feet and surveyed the street. There were few people in sight. The stone-laden wagon was turning into the construction site. An eagle floated across his line of vision. He looked at his shotgun and other items stacked beside the rocking chair.

He stepped down to the ground and crossed the street without hurrying.

"She's awake," Elizabeth said. "She tires easily. I hope you won't stay long."

"Just to pay my respects," Titus said. She was close to him and he smelled a sweet warmth and he remembered too well the long ago.

"She might not know you, Will."

"All right, I'm prepared. But I hope she does."

"Come on in, Will," she said and stood aside for him to enter.

He went through the door and took two more steps before he stopped, letting the memories rise as they would.

Elizabeth waited silently.

The big, open fireplace, with a window on each side. The organ on the opposite wall, tall, slim with small mirrors on the ornate backing, the ivory keys gleaming in the dimness of the large room.

The rocking chairs before the fireplace; he remembered the three of them, he and Bart and Elizabeth, sitting on the floor, watching the flames, listening to the desultory talk of the elders, his arm brushing Elizabeth's in a way that sent a glow all through him. He saw it all in the space of a few seconds and it was strange and yet old, as though this room may have been waiting for his return.

Elizabeth went past him. "We moved her downstairs into

the sewing and music room, Will." She went on and as he followed her, watching the movement of her body, he sternly put a lid on his thoughts and emotions. Somewhere in the distance a rooster crowed. He heard the sound of the rumble of wagon wheels on the bridge over the Troublesome.

The room was bright and cheerful, flooded with sunshine but it smelled of decay and death. The woman lying on the bed, beneath the patchwork quilt, with her eyes closed, sent a shock all through him.

Her hair, once auburn and gleaming, was a thin brittle gray, sparse; her face emaciated, shrunken, almost a skull, her skin taut and yellowed.

She opened her eyes.

He breathed a small sigh of inward thanks.

Only her eyes were unchanged, the gentle brown he remembered, clear and alive. She raised a clawlike hand from the multicolored patchwork quilt. "Bart," she whispered in an almost inaudible voice.

Elizabeth said, "Mama, he's not Bart. It's Will Titus." She looked at Titus. "You may kiss her cheek, Will. It's not contagious."

Titus approached the bed and took Martha's hand. It was cold, lifeless. He leaned over and brushed his mustache against her cheek.

She clutched his hand with surprising strength. "Will, Will! You were always a good boy. Bring Bart home, just once. I want to see him before I die."

"Ma'am, I don't know where Bart is," Titus said, remembering this woman as she had been, tucking him into his bed, when he was young, bending over him, the sweet smell of her warming him, as she covered his shoulders, leaning down to kiss him good night.

"Don't call me ma'am," she whispered. And then: "You were always so good at doing things, Will. You can let him know. If Bart only knows he'll be here. He will come if he can."

He stood there, holding her hand, a confusion of feelings fighting for possession of his emotions, his senses. The fight inside him was not strong enough to blot out his instincts; nor the faint shadow moving across the window behind him. There was someone there.

He released her hand, stepped to the right, motioning Elizabeth away from him, propelling her against the far wall out of the range of possible gunfire. He placed his right hand on the upright of the four-poster bed and reached for the shoulder gun under his right arm with his left hand.

He could see nothing but fruit trees through the window but suddenly the window glass flew inward, coinciding with the roar of a shotgun.

CHAPTER 7

A muzzle-loader, Titus thought, standing to one side of the window, holding the .38 in his left hand but with no target in sight.

He pressed forward with the pistol cocked. He fired at a waving bush beyond the trees and heard a cry of pain and shock.

Titus peering cautiously around the edge of the window and the shotgun roared again, showering remaining fragments of window glass into the room.

"In God's name, Will, stop it!" Elizabeth screamed.

Titus stood beside the window, holding the pistol, staring down at Martha Laney, still, her eyes closed, her hands clutching the quilt.

Elizabeth leaned against the wall, her clenched fist pressed against her mouth, her eyes wide, frightened.

Doctor McNair plunged through the door and froze there, staring at Martha and then turning his eyes on Titus. "It's come to this," he said quietly. He was hatless, wearing a bandage tinged with pink spots on his head.

Thomas P. Riley came in more slowly, mumbling as though repeating some secret ritual.

"Get out there, Constable," Titus ordered. "Somebody just tried to kill me."

"That's your problem, Marshal," Riley left off his mutterings to say. "I ain't about to get tangled up in it."

Without another word, Titus stepped past the doctor and constable and left the house. He went directly to the area where the ambusher had made an attempt on his life. He found a double-barreled shotgun, an ancient muzzle-loader with 36-inch barrels. He picked it up, hefting it, and put it over his shoulder. He found footprints in the soft soil of the orchard leading away from the house, the long strides indicating a man running hard. He found a drop of blood on a green leaf from the plum tree.

He followed the tracks to the back of the orchard, where morning glory vines formed a fence. The ambusher had apparently leaped this fence.

"Wasn't hurt too bad or he couldn't have jumped that," Titus muttered to himself. He went around the fence and came back to where the ambusher had landed after the jump. There were no traces of blood there. He thought: just nicked him. He lost the trail in the hard ground beyond the fence.

Jason Gardner was scared out of his wits. He admitted it to himself, as he ran blindly from Laney's fruit orchard.

He'd acted out of the pact he'd made with George Fenton, a pact he'd tried to forget when Titus killed George. Jason and George had agreed that one of them would get Titus.

George had died because of that pact and now, he, Jason had nearly bought a six by four foot plot in the local graveyard.

That thought was what scared him beyond coherent action.

It was not until he jumped the morning glory fence that he realized he'd dropped the shotgun. He didn't remember.

He thought: to hell with the shotgun. Nobody knew where it come from, anyway. George had stolen it from a Gentile farmer up in Paiute Valley.

George had found the buffalo gun beside the skeleton of some wandering miner, trapper or mountain man, who met death in a manner unknown to any local. Everybody in town knew about George Fenton's buffalo gun. No one knew of the double-barreled muzzle-loader.

Jason had pretended to his mother that George's death

didn't matter, that George wasn't really his best friend. It didn't work. He did grieve for George.

He'd lied about that and now God was punishing him for it. He was alive, however, with a crease of a bullet on his upper arm. It was hardly more than a scratch and had stopped bleeding almost as soon as he stopped running, out of breath, his side hurting fiercely, in Cantrell's barn.

He stared around the small room that had been George's living quarters, built in a corner of the barn and always smelled of hay and horses and leather.

Jason admitted that George had always been sort of strange. George had funny ideas, but Jason had envied him his freedom, his living quarters in Cantrell's barn, his uncanny luck in finding things, such as the guns and all that. George came and went as he pleased as long as he did the chores Cantrell imposed on him in return for food and shelter.

The impulse to kill Titus had come suddenly, as he saw the marshal crossing the street to the Laney home. Jason knew the layout of the house and he thought it would be easy.

He got the shotgun from under a loose board in the floor of the small corner room in the barn. He barely considered the consequences of his act as he checked the shotgun with the ramrod and found it fully loaded. Maybe overloaded, as the loading notch in the hickory rod was at least a half-inch above the end of the long twin barrel.

There were no firing caps and he searched feverishly for the small tin box until he uncovered it under a piece of fur from a muskrat.

Selecting two caps he placed them over the nipples under the twin hammers. He went out the back way, wending his way through the orchards until he came to the Laney house. He could hear Lucian's hammer ringing on the anvil as he squatted beside a plum tree.

He didn't have to wait at all. He saw the tall marshal standing inside the window, with his hand on the bedpost. He sighted in the long-barreled shotgun and to keep it from wavering, braced it against the trunk of the plum tree, over the waist-high weeds. Shutting one eye, he saw the broad shape appear centered under the ivory bead, and pulled the trigger. He must have closed his eyes when he pulled the trigger. He heard the sound of the shotgun, a roaring that hurt his ears, he heard the sound of tinkling glass. He opened his eyes and didn't see the marshal.

The kick of the shotgun almost broke his shoulder. He next knew the sharp sting on his left arm and the sharp spiteful report of the marshal's pistol.

He almost fled then, but the glimpse of the marshal at the edge of the window was too much. He fired the second barrel.

The marshal's hat was visible and part of his face. Jason lost his nerve, threw the gun down and fled in terror, expecting any moment to feel the burn of a bullet in his back.

Titus stood for a time on the back side of the orchard, his narrowed glance swinging here and there. Jenny watched motionless from the doorway across the road. He came at a leisurely pace around the end of the morning glory vine fence, jumping a shallow irrigation ditch, passing the chained Shagrun, who muttered an obscenity.

Lucian came from the smithy carrying a toolbox. He placed it on the ground when he saw Titus.

"I'm fixin' to fix Martha's window," he said, surveying the marshal with cold, unfriendly eyes. "Ain't right for a dyin' woman, a good woman, to go through all that, Will."

"I agree," Titus said.

Shagrun shouted, "You gonna keep me like this, chained up like some damn animal?"

"You'll get used to it," Titus said.

"Damn you," Shagrun raged, "I ever get a chance I'll—"

"You have a very small chance," Titus said and swung the muzzle-loader off his shoulder and held it out for Lucian's inspection. "Ever see this before?"

The blacksmith looked at the gun critically, shaking his head. "I know most guns hereabouts," he said. "I fix them, too, you know; we ain't had a gunsmith since ol' Link Perry died a few years back. I ain't never laid eyes on that gun before. Only man I know owns one similar is—no, his'n has a 32-inch barrel and that'n is 36."

"Just thought I'd ask," Titus said, and turned away, ignoring Shagrun's muttered curses.

He placed the shotgun beside his pile of belongings on Grafton's front porch and resumed his seat in the rocking chair.

Grafton came home from the store at dusk and with a curt "Good evenin'," went on into the house. Titus could hear the sound of Grafton's and Jenny's voices but could not make out what was being said.

Jenny came out with a bowl in her hand. She had her bonnet tied in place. "Here's some venison stew," she said and gave him the bowl. "I'm going home now. Good night, Marshal."

"Thank you," he said, accepting the bowl. "Good night, Jenny."

He watched her step down and walk away, disappearing soon in the falling dusk. He felt a twinge of loneliness.

Titus ate half the bowl of stew and set the bowl on the floor. He walked around the house and picked up a wooden bucket he'd noted earlier and filled it with water from the well. He went back, got the bowl half-filled with stew and crossed the road.

Shagrun was slumped against the snubbing post. Lucian had completed the window repairs and gone home.

"Food and water," Titus said briefly and placed the bucket and bowl on the ground, within Shagrun's reach.

He went back to the front porch and sat down. There were few lights in town that he could see. These people were frugal, he well knew. They geared their living to night and day, saving candles and coal oil.

He sat there in the darkness, listening to the sounds of Grafton getting ready for bed. He stilled the rocking chair and sat quietly, hearing the pad of feet crossing and recrossing the room, the clank of the lid on the chamber pot, the creak of bed springs.

Then, all was quiet, except for the hooting of an owl in the far distance, the sharp barking of a dog nearer, a bark ending on a yelp and then silence.

He started rocking again, slowly, so other sounds could come to him. The Laney home was dark. A streak of yellow light flowed through the front windows of the boot and saddle shop and added a golden glow to the silvery dust of the road. The mountains in the east seemed carved out of black cardboard. He picked out the peaks he knew. The dip called Paiute Pass, more a dip than a pass, where he'd killed his first deer. Or was it where Bart got *his* first deer?

The sky up to the edge of the porch roof was visible, filled with stars that seemed near. Nowhere in the world had he found the sky so vivid as in this wild and savage country.

Compensation of a sort, he thought.

Titus stilled his motion again at a distant sound. He unconsciously alerted his senses, and then relaxed as Elizabeth emerged from the shadows and crossed the road. He knew her immediately, from the shape of her, the way she carried herself, even in the shadowy night.

She came through the yard and sat on the edge of the porch leaning her back against the rough timber that supported the roof.

She looked at the outline of him, a big man so sure of himself that it bordered on arrogance. Where had he been all the years past? What had he done? What did he think?

She knew she had loved him in their youth and she thought he had loved her. But over all those years, no word from him, except after he became famous for his exploits, when something would be reported in the weekly newspaper that frequently arrived two weeks after it was printed in Salt Lake.

Almost as if reading her thoughts he said, "I keep remembering all that happened here. I felt like I was coming home but it didn't happen. Eagerness, maybe. And something else I can't put to words."

She stirred restlessly. "Will, what happened all these years? Are you the same man as the boy who left?"

Titus chuckled. "Not at all. When I left here with my uncle I was all broke up. I didn't want to go. He was a stranger. I was leaving my real folks.

"I tried to slip away a couple of times. But he was a mighty sweet-talking man and by the time we got on the train at Ogden he had me eating out of his hand. And believing every word he said."

He stopped talking and she waited. While she was fearful of his reason for being there, something different from fear was also there but eluded her.

He went on, "By the time we got to Arkansas, I knew my uncle pretty well and didn't like what I'd learned. He was a violent man, given to insane rages. And he painted a bloody picture of what had happened to my parents, my older sister and all those others who were slaughtered like cattle, and then robbed. For it was a wealthy wagon train, good animals, the best, good rolling stock. There was gold and silver and other valuables. My uncle told me that was the real reason the emigrants were wiped out."

Bats dipped, swooped and darted about in the cool night sky, and small clouds, dissipating, breaking up, drifted overhead. The chair creaked as he stirred restlessly.

He was close to her, stirring the yearnings she'd repressed over the years. She sensed that this man was far removed from the youth she'd known and loved.

The thought gave her a sadness that went even deeper than the sadness for her outlaw brother and dying mother.

"Will, Will, I wish you'd never come. But somehow I'm glad you're here, now that you are."

"I've brought you trouble for which I'm sorry."

"Yes."

He was close to her. She smelled the soap he'd used recently, the smell of gun oil, horse and leather and tobacco that soap couldn't eradicate. Memories flooded her mind of a Sunday afternoon in Shapp's barn, when there were only the two of them. Her face burned as she wondered if he remembered, too.

"Remember Shapp's barn?" he asked.

Startled, she blurted, "I was thinking of it."

"I've thought about it and dreamed about it and lived it over a thousand times," he said. He was trying again to recapture it in a border brothel when his right wrist was cut.

Elizabeth had been his first and only love; and it was in Shapp's barn, now Lucian Bowman's blacksmith shop, when he was sixteen that they found theirs was not a brother-sister love.

"It could be that way again," she said, forcing herself to talk in that manner.

There was a pain inside him like he'd never known. He said roughly, "There's no way I'll leave without Bart. If he comes here."

"All those years with us, you, one of us, doesn't it mean anything to you?"

He thought: I never think about that. If I did maybe something would happen I don't want to happen. Why do I try to close out part of what I am? "Yes," he said.

Suddenly, desperately, Elizabeth searched for words that would move him, words to make him abandon his relentless search, words that would make him part of her again.

Also, she knew suddenly and with a feeling of despair that it would never be so.

"Good night, Will," she said, and was gone.

He sat there, still, feeling her presence, wondering how it was that the warm pleasant feeling he'd had for such a little while was gone.

He suddenly wished that he was back in Tucson.

He wished again that he'd never heard of Circle Valley.

"I'm a goddamned fool," he muttered to himself and picked his bedroll out of the pile of duffle and went to a spot under the poplar tree he'd selected earlier.

CHAPTER 8

In the early morning hours the sound of horsemen aroused Titus. He followed the approach of the cavalcade, cradling his shotgun. After the group passed, he rose from his bedroll, folded it, and after a visit to the creek, returned to his watch on the front porch of Grafton's house. The horsemen had continued south and he estimated there were six of them, walking their animals, riding in silence.

Jenny Gardner came earlier than usual and he watched her approach with a critical though appreciative eye. A most seemly woman, he thought, and not for the first time.

He stopped his rocking motion as she mounted the steps, removing her sunbonnet even though the sun had not cleared the mountain as yet. She reached into her apron pocket and brought out a slip of paper.

"Jason brought this from Doctor McNair," she said. "It's for you."

She watched him as he unfolded the sheet of paper and scanned it.

> Marshal (the note read) I'm indisposed or I'd deliver this in person. Watch carefully for a man built like an ape with knuckles sweeping the ground. His right arm is in splints. Beware, for hidden by the splints and bandages is a .41 derringer and I think he means to kill you.
>
> Doctor M.

Titus glanced up. "You read this?" he asked.

She gave him a contemptuous look. "It is not meant for me," she said. "It is no business of mine."

He thrust the note into his vest pocket. "Women are notable for their curiosity," he said and seeing her quick frown, added quickly, "so I've been told."

"You may be right," she said tartly, moving toward the door. His voice stopped her.

"Should you see a man with his arm in a sling, absent yourself and stay in a safe place."

"Trouble collects around you whether there's a man with his arm in a sling or not."

"It seems that way at times. By the way, there were riders early this morning, heading south."

"So?"

"I wondered what it meant, if anything special."

"You should know everything that goes on if you're so insistent on making a target of yourself on Brother Grafton's front porch."

"I'd like to be able to say that I know everything that goes on. But, no, that's beyond me. Who were those riders and where were they headed?"

She smiled a sly smile. "Your fellow marshals would like that information." Seeing the wrinkle on his forehead, she added: "Those marshals are looking for what they call bigamists."

"So they were men going to visit their secret wives, or coming from a visit?"

"They have their obligations, too."

"Ah, well, it's of no concern to me. Not at this time."

"You'd be much safer chasing men with more than one wife."

He nodded agreement. "Safety is not a factor in the way I do business."

"Then you're a bigger fool than I thought." She wheeled about and whisked inside.

Titus smiled faintly. Jenny Gardner was one hell of a

woman. He wondered briefly why she seemed so concerned about his welfare and then dismissed the thought as he took McNair's note from his vest pocket and read it again.

Later, he focused his attention on a cloud of gray dust, approaching from the north. As the team and vehicle neared, it slowed, and out of the dust emerged a gleaming six-passenger rockaway with red wheels and pulled by a team of matched grays. A black driver hauled back on the reins. A man in a white panama hat opened the door and stepped to the ground and looked up and down the road. He then looked at Titus.

"Marshal Will Titus?"

Relaxing slightly, Titus nodded.

"I'm Samuel L. Clemens, better known as Mark Twain."

Titus' eyes flickered. He stiffened and leaned forward in his chair, a sharp watchfulness on his face. "Is that so?"

The man nodded, smiling. He came up the steps and offered his hand to Titus.

Titus ignored the proffered hand, staring intently at the man claiming to be Mark Twain.

The man, a short, brown-eyed individual with black hair stepped away and to do something with his rejected hand removed his hat. "The stonemason down there building the church said I'd find you here."

"Yep. Here I am."

The man removed a cigar case from an inside coat pocket and opening it, offered Titus a cigar.

Titus had exhausted his supply of tobacco on his long ride from the south. He hungered for a smoke but shook his head in refusal.

"I was in San Francisco a few years back," Titus said. "I paid good money to listen to Mark Twain lecture. You're not the man I listened to, mister. What's your game?"

The man stood there with the cigar poised between his fingers close to his open mouth, frozen for a long, pregnant moment. He deliberately bit off the end of his cigar, turning his head to spit out the tip. Clenching his teeth around the cigar, he struck a match on the wooden post and lit his smoke.

"No game, really, Marshal," he said between puffs. "I thought I'd find my way easier by pretending to be Twain. My name is Bret Horn. Maybe you've heard of me?"

"No."

"I'm a journalist, work for the *Times-Democrat*."

"Never heard of that either," Titus said. "You said pretending to be Twain would make it easier for you. Easier for what?"

"To write a story about you, Marshal."

"Is that what you usually write about?"

"I do exposé sort of articles—sensationalism is what I strive for."

"And you're comparable to Twain?"

"No, no. I'm a better writer than Twain. He's simply better known than me."

Titus rose and stretched. "What is it you want from me?"

"As I said, I want to do an article on the famous Marshal Will Titus. In his environment, a perfect environment for the kind of man you are."

"How could you know what kind of man I am?"

"I found out a good deal about you before I set out on this project. I talked to your superior, Chief Marshal Eldon Flagle in Washington, D.C., a man familiar with your background."

Flagle talks too much, Titus thought. He nodded toward the rockaway standing on the side of the road. "Where'd you get the fancy rig?"

"Rented it from a Mormon bishop at the end of the railroad." Surveying the surrounding country, he exclaimed, "Thunderation, what a desolate land. What in hell is it good for?"

"To hold the world together, I reckon. The people here raise cattle and lots of kids."

Horn smiled delightedly. "To hold the world together," he repeated, savoring the words. "I should have said that, Marshal. You not only are an efficient law officer but you can turn a phrase. I'd better watch my laurels."

"You've nothing to worry about from me," Titus said. "Unless you break a federal law, such as crossing territorial lines while impersonating a famous writer."

Horn whipped out a notebook and pencil. "I am a writer and a good one, Marshal. I had a momentary lapse of judgment. Everyone is allowed at least one small error." Making a few rapid notes, he scribbled: Remarkably handsome man, virile, over six feet tall, about 200 pounds, coldest blue eyes I've ever seen—softspoken, polite, but a touch of steel lurks underneath—rather broad across cheeks, thin lips beneath black mustache—can this be the famous marshal reputed to have killed six or sixteen notorious outlaws?

Glancing up from his notes, Horn asked: "What say you, Marshal? You want to help me write a dandy story about you?"

"Fellow name of Buntline wanted to do that," Titus said. "I wasn't interested then, nor am I interested now."

"My work is on a somewhat more literary level than that of Buntline," Horn said stiffly.

"I'll make a deal with you," Titus said thoughtfully.

Horn's face brightened. "What kind of deal?"

"You've heard of the Circle Valley Massacre?"

Horn nodded.

"You should know the truth if anybody does."

Horn wrinkled his brow and puffed on his cigar. "I heard three different stories. One, Indians massacred a hundred and twenty men, women and children in a Gentile wagon train traveling through this country, over east of this very spot; two, Gentiles blamed it on the Mormons. Story number three was that Indians were partly to blame, Mormons partly to blame, and the wagon train brought it on itself. It was not until several years after I heard those stories that I got what come out of the federal trial. I know full well that Matthew Laney and his Mormon cohorts were totally responsible. Why are you interested, Marshal?"

"I was one of the seven children that survived," Titus said. He stiffened suddenly and leaned forward, speaking softly: "Mr. Horn, don't ask questions. Just get up and go casually to your rockaway and drive down the road a hundred feet or so and wait. Stay inside the coach."

Without waiting for Horn's response he slipped off the end of the porch and circled the house, moving swiftly. Going past the back door Jenny Gardner stepped outside.

"Shush!" he said as she opened her mouth to speak. "Get back inside."

He went on, drawing the .38 from his shoulder rig; he came to the north side of Grafton's house and caught a glimpse of the man Doc had warned him of, crossing the road to turn into the yard.

Titus slid along the side of the building, taking care not to brush against the house. He stepped softly around the end of the porch with his pistol leveled.

"Stand still, you murderin' sonofabitch," Titus said. He noted that Horn was standing beside the rockaway, staring at him. He thought: let the dumb sonofabitch stay there and get shot for all of me.

Shoving the .38 back into the shoulder rig, Titus stepped ahead and a slim blade appeared in his left hand. He took two more swift steps forward, and said: "Stand still, Gorila." He reached over the man's shoulder and Gorila shrank away from the knife and then froze.

The blade flashed and the sling and splints on Gorila's right arm fell to the ground.

Titus removed the .41 over-and-under derringer from Gorila's shaking hand.

He prodded Gorila in the back with the derringer and said, "Start walking. Head for the blacksmith shop."

Gorila stuttered, "Señor, they tol me you didn't know me. I mean you no harm—"

Titus silenced him with a light tap on the head with the derringer. "I know all about you, you murderin', thievin' rapist. I
learned about you when you raped that ten-year-old girl in
Cortaro and murdered her mother. I got a poster on you."

"I nev' been to Cortaro," Gorila protested. "Whas a poster?"

"A piece of paper," Titus said, "with your picture on it."

Gorila stumbled into the area before the blacksmith shop.
Lucian came from the smithy, his leather apron flapping
around his sturdy legs. "What now, Will?"

"Put leg irons on him and bolt him to your snubbing post,"
Titus said. "Right alongside the other one."

Shagrun, who had been dozing with his back against the
snubbing post, raised his head. When he saw Titus he yelled:
"How long you gonna keep me chained up like this, Marshal?
It ain't human."

Titus didn't answer Shagrun but nodded to Lucian. "Get on
with it, Lucian. You'll get paid for it."

"The gov'ment's mighty slow about payin'," he said.

"You can use some hard dollars. Might take a little time but
it's worth it."

Lucian nodded, turned, began searching a scrap bin for
chain and iron.

Shagrun shouted again: "You gonna let me starve or die of
thirst? You gonna let me lie here and die, is that what you're
gonna do?"

"You'll live long enough to stretch rope." Titus shoved
Gorila toward the snubbing post. "Set there beside that one."

When Gorila was slumped beside Shagrun, Titus slipped the
derringer into his side pocket and headed back to Grafton's
front porch.

Horn was waiting on the porch when Titus resumed his seat
in the rocking chair. Titus lifted the Winchester and placed it
across his knees. He levered the action back far enough to
check the load. There was a round in the firing chamber. He
kept the rifle across his knees, his eyes on the two men at the
snubbing post in front of the smithy.

Horn said thoughtfully, "I've been in this country several times. I can't see much change during the years since my first time here."

"I can agree with that."

"Is there anything I can say or do that will help you make up your mind to cooperate with me?"

"I've made my position known."

"Ah, indeed. But a reasonable man can change his mind."

"If I was a reasonable man I might not be here."

Horn laughed. "I've got to admire the way you operate even if I feel defeated. I spent a lot of time and money to come out here and try for the story of the decade."

"That's the chance you take in your business."

"At least it's not fatal," Horn said lightly. His expression grew serious. "I've researched the Circle Valley Massacre. I have an authentic report from a lady who was present at the trial held in Salt Lake City. You may care to look at it."

"Thanks. But I'm not apt to change my mind."

Horn made no reply but made his way to the rockaway. Titus watched the vehicle circle in the road in front of Grafton's house. He watched it until it disappeared in a cloud of gray dust raised by its passage.

CHAPTER 9

Later Titus picked up the papers left by Bret Horn. He read through them, looking up at intervals to make certain he missed nothing.

According to witnesses, a revelation from the President of the Church of Jesus Christ of Latter-Day Saints, was dispatched to Matthew Laney, commanding him to raise all the forces he could muster and trust, to follow those cursed Gentiles, attack them while the attack forces are disguised as Indians, and with the arrows of the Almighty make a clean sweep of them, and leave none to tell the tale; and if they need any assistance Laney was commanded to hire the Indians as their allies, promising them a share of the booty. They were to be neither slothful nor negligent in their duty, and to be punctual in sending the teams back before winter set in, for this was the mandate of Almighty God.

The command was faithfully obeyed. A large party of Mormons, painted and tricked out as Indians, overtook the train of emigrant wagons some three hundred miles south of Salt Lake City, and made an attack. But the emigrants threw up earthworks, made fortresses of their wagons and defended themselves gallantly and successfully for five days.

At the end of the five days the Mormons tried military strategy. They retired to the upper end of the valley, resumed civilized apparel, washed off their paint, and then heavily armed, drove down in wagons to the beleaguered emigrants, bearing a flag of truce. When the emigrants saw white men coming they welcomed them with cheer after cheer. And, all unconscious of the duplicity, they lifted a little child aloft, dressed in white in answer to the flag of truce.

Laney professed to be on good terms with the Indians, and represented them as being angry. He also proposed to intercede and settle the matter with the Indians. After several hours parley, they, having supposedly visited the Indians, gave the ultimatum of the savages; which was, that the emigrants should march out of their camp, leaving everything behind them, even their guns. It was promised by Laney that he would bring a force and guard the emigrants back to the settlements. The terms were agreed to, the emigrants being desirous of saving the lives of their families. The Mormons retired, and subsequently appeared with thirty or forty armed men. The emigrants were marched out, the women and children in front and the men behind, the Mormon guard being in the rear. When they had marched in this way about a mile, at a given signal the slaughter commenced. The men were almost all shot down at the first fire from the guard. Two only escaped, who fled to the desert, and were followed one hundred and fifty miles before they were overtaken and slaughtered. The women and children ran on, two or three hundred yards farther, when they were overtaken and with the aid of the Indians they were slaughtered. Seven individuals only, of the emigrant party, were spared, and they were little children, the eldest of them being seven years old. Thus, on the 10th day of September, 1857, was consummated one of the most cruel, cowardly and bloody murders known in history.

Titus sighed. What in hell could a man believe? The lady
who had written the report was an ex-wife of one of the men
on trial with Matthew Laney.

That's one way to get even, he thought. But there was more
truth in this report than in the clipping in Elmer Grafton's general store.

Titus was nervous. When Jenny came out the door pinning
on her Sunday hat, he was tense and even jumpy.

He relaxed and watched her finish, noting how infinitely
feminine her movements were.

"I'm off to George Fenton's funeral," she said.

He did not reply.

The undertaking parlor and cemetery were on the north end
of town but he'd noted the numbers of people passing Grafton's house from the south, dressed in Sunday finery, walking
past, riding in buckboards, buggys, surreys and just about
every kind of vehicle imaginable. All of them avoided looking
at him as they passed.

Finally he said, "I'm sorry I'm unable to attend."

She looked at him for long moments with her beautiful
amber eyes glowing. Then without speaking she walked down
the steps. She paused there, turned, and said: "If you see
Jason tell him to get himself to church."

She crossed to the worn path beside the road and walked
north and he watched until she disappeared around the gentle
turn of the road beyond Grafton's store.

He knew the people in town thought him foolhardy for
displaying himself on Grafton's front porch. He was not concerned with what the townspeople thought. He was aware that
he wasn't safe but what bothered him more was that he wasn't
free. He was chained to that spot, to await the coming of Bart
Laney.

He displayed himself in the hope that Laney would see him
and sense a challenge and take it up.

Titus lifted his eyes to the mountains and scanned them

from right to left, searching for movement. Up there, the brooding mountains could contain a thousand men and not a million searchers could find them.

So he would wait and take his chances. That was what the government paid him to do.

Jason slipped around the corner to find the twin barrels of the shotgun trained on his belly.

"Don't sneak up on me like that," Titus said.

"Warn't sneakin', just warn't thinkin'," Jason whined.

"Your mother said for you to come to the funeral."

"I don't wanna go," Jason said in a sullen voice.

"Why not, wasn't he your friend?"

"Nah. George was crazy. I mean looney. Touched in the head."

"I get your meaning," Titus said dryly.

"So why should I go to his funeral?"

"That's up to you except you should respect the wishes of your mother. You're not of age yet."

"Aw, she don't know nothin'."

Titus stood the shotgun on end and stepped down and took Jason by the front of his shirt and lifted him to the tips of his boots.

"You go wash your face and get the hell down to that church," he said savagely, "or I'll whip the daylights out of you."

Jason's teeth were chattering. "Yes, sir," he gasped and Titus released him. He wheeled and trotted away, now and then looking over his shoulder.

Titus resumed his vigil in the rocking chair. He could hear the music from the ward house, where the funeral was being held. Then the sound of voices joined the music. The words were from an old song he remembered from his youth. He hummed it, under his breath, *Yes, we'll gather at the river, that flows by the throne of God . . .*

That was all of it he could remember.

Gust Bogan and Manta Kile tied their horses in a clump of mahogany and walked toward the rim of the canyon where the Mormons quarried rock to build their new church.

As they neared the edge, Gust dropped to his hands and knees and motioned Kile to do likewise.

Together, they crawled toward the rim and before peering over the ridge Bogan removed his sweat and grease-encrusted hat and placed it on the ground beside him. He reached out and ripped off Kile's hat and jammed it in the smaller man's hands with a muttered curse.

Two men worked, carrying stone to the wagon. Six oxen were tethered on a rope stretched along the vari-colored canyon wall, munching hay that had been spread along the picket line. A yellow dog lay in the sun near the oxen but not near enough to be stepped on.

"Good," Bogan grunted, snaking backward from the rim. "Just two o' them."

When they were far enough away from the rim to be detected, Bogan rose. He glowered at Kile, "You got it all straight in your head?"

Manta Kile nodded, getting slowly to his feet. "Yep."

"All right, then, let's go down there."

In the canyon, Ephraim and Moroni Riley loaded stone blocks. Grubbs, the stonemason, had provided the quarry crew with a block of wood the size of stone he desired, warning them that the tolerance could be no more than two inches.

The size of the quarrying crew varied because the volunteers could only work when they had time off from other work. Moroni had explained patiently to Ephraim that they'd load the wagon and then go on to George Fenton's funeral, returning to bring the wagon load of stone to the church after the funeral.

Moroni was the exact image of Thomas P. Riley, the constable, squat, powerful, dark, and with a good mind. He was a good worker, as was Ephraim.

Ephraim was simpleminded and had to be directed in almost every single task he undertook. Moroni had lots of patience for his brother and seldom grew angry when the tall one blundered, which was often unless closely supervised.

Ephraim was chipping away with a stonemason's tool when Bogan and Kile rode in with their pistols ready.

The two Mormons stopped working, straightened and stared. Neither brother was armed.

The yellow dog raised his head, growled once, and slumped back to the ground, losing all interest in the new arrivals.

"You fellers keep right on workin'," Bogan said. "Jes' don't put no rock in the middle of the waggin. Leave a hole there big enough fer me to get inter." He held out his two hands, one of which held a .44 Colt. "About this here size. "An' somethin' else. On the lef' hand side I want a crack about two-three inches, so's I kin get my rifle bar'l through it, see?"

Ephraim, a look of alarm on his face, moved closer to Moroni and Bogan cocked his pistol.

"Nothin' funny," he said, "or I'll blow a hole in yore belly."

"He's afraid," Moroni said to Bogan, looking at Ephraim. "Don't fret Ephraim. We'll be all right."

"If'n you do what you're told, you crazy sumbitches," Bogan said. "Now, get to it!"

He dismounted and handed his reins to Kile. "Tie 'em up over by the oxen," he said. "Them pore damn hosses ain't had a square meal in a month o' Sundays."

Kile obediently rode his own horse and led Bogan's horse to the picket line and tied them to the rope. The horses began munching hay hungrily.

Kile squatted in the shade of the canyon wall nearby. Soon, Bogan came over. The two of them watched silently as the Riley brothers toiled at loading the wagon.

Working faster than usual, the wagon was soon loaded. The brothers stood back and looked at the duo lounging in the shade.

"It's done," Moroni announced.

Bogan leisurely rose to his feet and looked at Kile, nodding. The two men walked to the wagon.

"Hey, wait a minute," Kile said. "Better let them hitch up them damn oxen first. I ain't never done it."

Bogan was irritated. The idea should have occurred to him first.

"Well, I know how," he said. "Let's get this over with."

Bogan motioned at Moroni and Ephraim. "Turn around, fellers," he ordered. "Face t'other way."

Moroni turned slowly, grabbing Ephraim by the arm to turn the tall man.

When the Mormon brothers were facing away, Bogan and Kile stepped forward and brought their guns crashing down on the unprotected heads.

Bogan hit Moroni and Kile hit Ephraim.

Moroni dropped in his tracks but Ephraim turned, blood running down his face, bewildered, crying out: "Don't hurt me, don't hurt me!"

The yellow dog sprang to his feet and began barking. Kile aimed his pistol at the dog.

"Don't shoot, Kile, you crazy bastid!" Bogan shouted and began clubbing Ephraim. He struck again and again until the lanky youth was sprawled on the ground.

Bogan holstered his pistol and looked around until he found a rock of the right size. He lifted it in his two hands and kneeling over the senseless Moroni hammered at his head with the rock. He knee-walked to Ephraim and did the same thing. He stood up and threw the rock from him.

He got a handful of small rocks and threw them at the barking dog, driving the animal up the canyon and out of sight. Without looking at the two brothers he went to the tethered oxen and began to yoke them up. He led them, by two's to the wagon and hitched them.

When he was finished, Bogan climbed the pile of stones and disappeared into the square hole the brothers had made as directed.

His head appeared. "Bring me my Winchester," he said.

Kile trotted to Bogan's horse and pulled the saddle gun from its scabbard and brought it to Bogan, handing it up butt first.

"All right, now," Bogan said. "All you gotta do is walk alongside the near wheeler after you get 'em movin', they'll go right along. They know the way."

"All right, Gust," Kile said in a scared voice.

"Where's the goddamned whip?" Bogan asked.

Kile looked around. "Oh, there it is on the double tree." He reached behind the near ox and retrieved the long, leather-plaited whip with a wooden handle. He looked up at Bogan. "Now, what's gee and haw agin?"

Bogan cursed roundly. "Hold up your right hand," he commanded.

"Aw, heck, Gust—"

"Hold up your goddamn right hand," Bogan shouted.

"All right, all right." Kile held up his right hand.

"That's gee. To turn 'em left you say haw, and you don't say it, you shout it, holler loud." He leaned down, glaring at Kile. "Got it?"

"Yeah, I guess," Kile muttered.

"You better not guess, you dumb sumbitch. An' don't cuss them goddamned oxen. They ain't used to cussin'."

Kile nodded.

"All right then. Move 'em out."

Kile cracked the whip and yelled, "Giddap!"

The yellow dog watched from behind a large boulder, softly growling. As the wagon pulled away the dog followed slowly, sometimes whimpering, sometimes growling.

CHAPTER 10

Restless, Titus sprang up and moved back and forth along the porch. He checked the shotgun, the Winchester, the Sharps and the double-barreled muzzle-loader. He removed the derringer from his pocket, the one he'd taken from Gorila, and inspected the wicked little two-shot weapon. Jamming it back in his pocket, he sat back down in the rocking chair and massaged his right wrist, flexing the fingers of his right hand.

Time passed. Jenny returned, flushed and perspiring.

"It was a beautiful service," she said, unpinning her hat, fluffing her hair as she stood beside the rocking chair.

"I told Jason to go to the service. Did he show up?"

"He came in before it was over. I declare that boy worries me to death. He snagged his arm on a piece of barbwire and it's getting infected."

The people returning from the funeral ebbed and flowed on the road in front of them. He watched without emotion as Elizabeth Laney turned into the Laney home without looking his way. What was she thinking, he wondered, what was she feeling? Why was it that his thoughts of her on the trail here were so different from what he now felt?

"When did that happen?" he asked Jenny.

She shook her head. "I don't know. I noticed it this morning, red and puffy and a little pus around the edges."

The clouds were drifting out over the valley. He felt the jumpiness return, intensified. He scanned the mountains beyond, the far reaches and lower levels and saw nothing. People were still moving along the road, afoot and in rigs and on horseback. He heard the sound of cloven hooves on the bridge and the rumble of the wagon. He heard a dog barking, sharp, incisive.

He thought: another load of stone for the church.

All his senses alerted, then. He grabbed the shotgun and pushed Jenny inside the door. "Stay inside."

The oxen plodded into view, followed by the yellow dog, now barking viciously and yet hanging back.

The Mormons wouldn't be hauling stone right after a funeral, he thought.

He stepped to the ground, apprehension gnawing at him, not for himself, but for the passing people: even though thinning out now, some were still around.

The wagon drew slowly abreast of him and he looked the load over suspiciously. He'd entertained the thought of Laney slipping in with a load of stone but had dismissed it as impractical.

Now Titus could see the crack between the stones; and the glint of gunmetal. He dropped the shotgun and reached for the Winchester and jumped down into the yard, landing solidly on the ground.

He caught a glimpse of Jenny's face at the door and shouted for her to take cover as a flash of fire and smoke came from the center of the load of stone. He felt the tug of the bullet with his head and his hat went sailing away as he brought the Winchester to his shoulder and fired at the aperture in the stone, just as another muzzle blast blazed at him.

Titus' .44–40 slug struck Bogan's jugular, severing the vein. Bogan stood up, blood spurting with each heartbeat, while he tried to lever another shell into his carbine.

Titus fired again, aware that people were wildly running and whipping their horses to get out of the line of fire. Women screamed, children cried and horses neighed. The dog came nearer and nearer, his teeth bared, snarling.

Titus' second shot caught Bogan just above his right eye. Bogan fell sideways across the stone, his rifle dropping to the ground.

Kile had his hands high in the air, shouting, "Don't shoot, don't shoot, I give up!"

Titus went swiftly across the road and prodded Kile in the back with his Winchester. "Get moving, little man," Titus said, leaning over to disarm Kile.

Titus kept prodding Kile with the muzzle end of his rifle and kept him off balance as he shoved Kile's pistol into his belt.

Lucian stood at the smithy door dressed in his Sunday best. "I'm just fresh from carryin' a boy to his grave," he said. "I'm not in a mind to talk to you, Marshal."

"It's not talk I'm after," Titus said.

"I know, I know," Lucian said. "You want me to chain up another one. Well, I ain't gonna do it, not in my Sunday best. You'll just have to wait till I get my work clothes on."

"That's fine with me," Titus said. He passed Kile's gun to Lucian who accepted it reluctantly. "Keep this on him while I fetch a pair of handcuffs from my duffle."

Recrossing the road, Titus caught sight of Jason standing at the end of Grafton's porch. He motioned to Jason.

Jason reluctantly came toward Titus, his eyes wide with fright.

"Drive the oxen on down to the church," Titus said. "Get the undertaker to take care of that man up there."

"Yes, sir," Jason croaked.

Titus leaned over and picked up the whip Kile had dropped on the ground and tossed it to Jason.

"You'll need that blacksnake," he said and went on to get a pair of handcuffs from his pack.

Jason snapped the whip and the oxen moved obediently down the road. Bogan's body rolled from side to side and Jason tried to avoid looking at it.

Titus returned to the smithy and handcuffed Kile to Lucian's anvil.

"I'll unlock him when you're ready for him," he told Lucian.

Lucian returned Kile's pistol to Titus without speaking and

went home through the orchard, to change into his work clothing.

"What's your name?" Titus asked.

"Kile. Manta Kile. Bogan made me do things for him. He'd kill if I didn't do what he said."

"That's the man on the wagon?"

"Yup. Gust Bogan." Kile began to whimper. "He's—"

"I know who he is," Titus said. "You're in bad and you're trying to squirm out. Now just settle down until Lucian chains you up along with those two."

Shagrun and Gorila stared owlishly at Titus; they said nothing and did not rattle their chains.

Titus returned to his watching post on Grafton's front porch.

He knew of the wild stories circulating in Circle City and not without cause. It was rumored that Jesse James, Wild Bill Hickok, Bat Masterson and Wyatt Earp were enroute either to lend Titus a helping hand or do him in.

Jenny Gardner emerged into the sun flooding the front porch and stood beside Titus' rocking chair.

"You should get plenty of fresh air to your head," she said tartly. "That man put a couple of holes through your hat."

He looked at her without speaking.

"It must be a horrible way to live," she went on, "never knowing what minute someone will try to gun you down."

"It's not the best way in the world to earn a living," he admitted.

She made a clucking sound.

"Don't cluck at me, woman," he said.

"I do declare, Will Titus—but what I want to tell you is this: Bishop Cantrell wants to talk to you."

"He knows where to find me."

"He doesn't want people to know he's talking to you."

"That figures. It'll be dark in a few hours. I'll be right here then."

"The Bishop says it can't wait. He's inside the house now. He'll talk through the window."

"I can't see a high and mighty bishop skulking around like a mangy coyote," Titus said.

"He's not skulking, as you call it," Jenny said. "I don't hold with the brothers but Bishop Cantrell is a good man doing the best he can in troublesome times."

"All right, you've made your speech. I'll hear what he has to say."

She whirled and with her shoulders stiffly erect marched into the house.

Will Titus heard the soft rumble of voices inside the house and then Bishop Cantrell spoke huskily from the window: "I hate to do this, Marshal, but things are getting out of hand."

"What is it you hate to do, Bishop?"

"Lay down the law."

"I'm the law."

"Not in this country."

"That's a question that's been settled long ago."

"Not entirely. I've held meetings with my counselors. Both of them agreed to my proposition. I've telegraphed President Cleveland and asked him to remove you from our town, to send you back to Arizona."

"President Cleveland will leave it up to the Chief of the U.S. Marshals, a man who has complete confidence in me."

Cantrell's voice lost whatever conciliation may have been present. "This was a quiet, peaceable town until you got here, Marshal. Four men are dead, two of them by your hand. The dregs of society flock in. Our people know no peace. I may have to call on the Danites."

"Your church has always denied the Danites, the Avenging Angels, the Destroying Angels, or whatever you call them."

"By whatever name, they are there in times of trouble," Cantrell declared. "If President Cleveland ignores my petition, I'll take whatever means available to rid this town and surroundings of undesirables."

"That might take a lot of doing," Titus said with a note of

finality in his voice. "I came here for a purpose and whatever happens I'll carry it off."

"Or die."

"We all do that sooner or later. Good day to you, Bishop Cantrell."

Stars were winking out over the La Sal Mountains when Bart Laney and Brace Bowman rode into the outlaw camp in a sparsely wooded canyon southwest of Circle City. Laney, a compactly built man, was fair looking with bleached out blond hair and green eyes and a ready grin. His sidekick, Brace Bowman, son of the village blacksmith, wore a derby which didn't conceal his flaming red hair. He also wore a double-breasted velvet vest under his fawn coat and pistol-legged pants rolled up to show his fancy boots with hand-stitching.

A small fire appeared ahead of them and Bowman blew out his breath gustily. "Damn glad we're here," he said. "Another day and I'd have blisters on my butt."

"We come a right fur piece," Laney said. He watched the campfire, appearing and disappearing as the trail followed the erratic contours of the mountain. He felt a growing sense of excitement at nearing home, an excitement that was quelled by his thoughts of his dying mother.

Laney's horse snorted and there was a motion around the campfire as Laney and Bowman emerged from the darkness and drew rein.

Ellie Bay raised himself on one elbow, grinning. "Hi, Bart, Brace." He crawled out from his bedroll and stood up, stretching and yawning. Two other men slept on undisturbed by the noise.

Laney dismounted stiffly and began loosening his saddle.

Ellie Bay came up alongside him and pushed him away. "Lemme do that," he said. "Go pour yourself a cup o' coffee. Bacon an' spuds in the fryin' pan."

Brace began unsaddling his own horse while Ellie took care of Laney's mount.

"How many men here?" Laney asked from a squatting position near the fire.

"There's them two there," Bay said, nodding to the mounded tarps on the other side of the fire. "Three more in the cabin."

"Which one is missing?" Laney dug into the frying pan with his fingers.

"Gorila."

"Where's he?"

Damn, here it comes, Ellie Bay thought with some dread. "He's down in Circle City, chained up to a snubbing post in front of Bowman's smithy."

Laney stopped eating and stood up. "What the hell you talkin' about?"

"Don't get your dander up, Bart," Ellie Bay advised. "I can explain—"

"Well, then, do it."

"I sent him down to kill Titus," Bay said doggedly. "I know what you said, but damn it, there ain't no other way, Bart."

Laney drew a bandanna from his hip pocket and began carefully wiping his hands. His features were indistinct in the flickering light of the camp fire.

Feeling uncomfortable, Bay went on: "Look, Bart, Titus hasn't been here a week and he's got two other men chained up along with Gorila, men who tried to kill him. He's set up watch on Grafton's front porch, across from your ma's house, and he's waitin' there for you. Ain't no way to move him outta there alive."

Laney's silence was threatening to Bay. He stripped off Laney's saddle and dumped it on the ground and began rubbing down the long-bodied, long-legged bay gelding.

"We'll manage," Laney finally said in a restrained tone. "Without killin' him, that is." He glanced at Bowman and then back to Ellie Bay. "I'm gonna catch some shuteye, Ellie. I'm plumb beat to a frazzle. When the boys wake up, keep 'em in camp 'til I've had my nap out."

"Fine, Bart. We done killed all the snakes around here so throw your soogan any ol' place."

"I ain't worried about snakes," Laney said. He looked at Bowman again. "Brace, I know you're just as tired as me but maybe you ought to ride down there and scout it out."

"Sure, Bart. I ain't really all that wore out. An' I do have a hankerin' to see my old man and my ma. It's been a long, long time."

Laney nodded and carried his bedroll away from the fire.

"You want to sleep under a roof," Ellie Bay called, "I'll roust out the ones sleepin' in the cabin."

"You know me better than that," Laney replied. "Sleepin' inside four walls is about the last thing I'd do."

"Yeah, I know. Thought I'd ask."

Laney disappeared and Ellie squatted beside the dying fire and looked across at Brace Bowman, squatting opposite him. "He didn't even mention his ma," he said.

"He don't mention a lot o' stuff," Brace said, "but he's still thinkin' about 'em." He shifted his weight back and forth and added: "Ellie, that was a damn fool thing to do, tryin' to kill Titus even when Bart said no."

"I was tryin' to do him a favor," Ellie grumbled.

"He don't want no kind of favor like that." He stood up. "I guess I better get movin'. I need a fresh horse."

Ellie rose and said, "I'll go fetch one," and strode off into the growing light, leading the weary horses Laney and Bowman had rode in on. He turned the horses into the rope corral beyond the cabin and caught up a rangy black. He brought the horse back to the fire. "I better find a dry saddle blanket. That one you been usin' is kinda wet."

"Yeah. We been ridin' nigh onto a week. What's new down in Circle City?"

"Outside Titus capturin' and chainin' up some pure puny bad actors, he's killed a couple an' caused the death of others, among them Riley's two sons."

"The hell you say."

"Yeah. An' then a feller calling himself Mark Twain come down to parley with Titus about writin' his life story or some such like that."

"Mark Twain? By ned, I'd better get down there and see for myself."

"Wasn't really Twain but an imposter, name of Horn. Titus put a gun on Gorila while Horn was there. That Horn feller lit out like a turpentined dog after that happened." He gave a final tug on the cinch and dropped the stirrup. "There y' are, Brace. Tell your ma hello for me."

Bowman swung up into the saddle. "I'll do that, Ellie." He rode down the mountain toward Circle City.

CHAPTER 11

Marshal Titus hailed Jason as the boy was passing on the road in front of Grafton's house. "Come here, boy."

Jason reluctantly turned back and shuffled to within ten feet of Titus. "What you want?" His voice quaked slightly.

Titus reached for the muzzle-loader and Jason gave a nervous jerk. "Ever see this gun before?" Titus asked.

Jason swallowed visibly, kicked hard at the ground with the toe of his worn boot. "No, sir."

"You didn't even look at it."

"I didn't have to, I don't hold with guns."

"Uh-huh, I see." Titus stood the gun back in place against the wall, rose and walked down the steps while alarm clouded Jason's eyes and face. "Come along, boy. I want to show you something."

Jason followed unwillingly. "I gotta get to work," he whined. "Mr. Grafton wants me to take some stuff to Bishop Cantrell's an—"

"That'll wait. Hurry along."

They passed the smithy and the orchard. Titus turned off the road and jumped the shallow irrigation ditch at the end of the orchard. He scanned the ground until he found the imprint of the boots of the person who'd fired the muzzle-loader at him through the Widow Laney's window. He stepped over the footprints and turned to face Jason.

"I want you to step in these boot tracks," Titus said, gesturing with his hand. "Come on, boy, don't stand there."

Jason took a step forward and stopped, his face pale, his

throat twitching. "I ain't gonna do it," he said through trembling lips.

"You shot at me," Titus said in a savage voice. "Shot at a United States marshal in pursuit of his sworn duty." His icy blue eyes never wavered from Jason's face as the boy stood trembling, twisting and finally thrusting his hands in his pockets.

"I—I—" He gulped and stopped speaking while tears welled up in his eyes and rolled down his cheeks.

"Well?"

"I didn't know what I was doing," Jason said miserably.

"You're old enough to know right from wrong."

"I do, I do. I knew 'twas wrong. I couldn't help myself."

"You better learn how to help yourself." Titus fought down his growing pity. He, too, was embarrassed, by Jason's abject terror.

Hope leaped into Jason's eyes as he sensed Titus' softening. "George talked me into it," he said. "I didn't want to, so help me. Then after George was—uh, killed, I figgered it was my duty. We'd made a pledge. I couldn't stop myself. What're you gonna do?"

"You'd better go home," Titus said. "I'll decide later if I'll chain you up with them murderers over there." He wheeled away. "I'll decide whether to charge you or not, based on your actions from here on in."

"Please don't chain me up," Jason pleaded. "I'll not do anything like that, not ever again, I swear!"

"All right. Go."

Jason broke into a hard run down the road. Jenny came from the house and called to him but he didn't respond to her command to come to her.

When Titus got back to his accustomed place on the front porch Jenny confronted him in vivid hostility, two bright red spots on her cheeks, her eyes bright with anger. "What's the matter with Jason?"

"You'd best ask him."

"He wouldn't stop when I called. He didn't even slow down. What'd you do to him, Will?"

He smiled at her and she realized with a start it was the first time she'd seen him smile. "Like most mammas you worry too much about your son," he said. "Leave him be and he'll do just fine."

"You make it sound too easy."

"Most people make things hard for themselves. They fool around and fool around with something real simple, trying to make it complicated." What he thought was that Jason had been scared out of his wits. That might turn him around. It was a hell of a serious matter trying to kill another human being. He had an idea that with Jenny for a mother Jason would come out all right.

"How old are you?" she asked suddenly.

"Oh, maybe thirty or so. I don't rightly know."

"Are you married or have you ever been?"

He shook his head negatively.

"How did you get so expert about kids if you've never had any?"

"I was a boy once." He flashed her a keen look. "Why do you ask? You got designs on me?"

She watched him with care, not rising to take the bait. "It seems a shame to me that you'll probably die right here on Brother Grafton's front porch and never know the delights of a good woman's love. And that of loving children."

He stopped rocking, his unseeing eyes on the distant mountains. His eyes cleared and he looked up at her. "I've not lived my life completely devoid of human relationships," he said dryly.

"There's something wrong with a man who reaches thirty and has never known a good woman's love."

"Oh, I've had a few experiences."

She flushed. "You would have, yes, a handsome man like you but was it—oh, oh, forgive me, Marshal, for running on like this. I don't know what's got into me here lately." She straightened her shoulders and half-turned away to watch a solitary horseman riding down the road past Grafton's store. The horseman came on, turning into Bowman's smithy. He wore a bowler hat and city clothes.

"It's Brace Bowman," she exclaimed, "come to visit his mother. Oh, she'll be so happy."

"Or coming home to scout for Bart."

"You'd do well to watch Brace," she warned. "He'd do anything in this world for Bart. Even kill a marshal."

"Yes, I believe he would," Titus said absently, watching Bowman dismount and shake hands with his father. The two men stood close together, talking. Now and then Lucian gestured toward Titus. Jenny quietly went into the house.

Titus didn't shift his position as Bowman crossed the road, leading his horse, a long-legged beautiful black with clean racing lines. Bowman ignored Gorila's plea to release him, not looking at the chained prisoners. He stopped a dozen feet from Titus, smiling at him as he lifted his bowler. His red hair blazed in the sun.

"Howdy, Marshal. I'm Brace Bowman."

"I know who you are," Titus said. "So you know Gorila?"

"Nah. Never seen him before."

"How long since you seen Bart?"

Bowman affected surprise. "Who, me? I ain't seen him— well, I did have a little talk with Bart over Colorado way when he found out I was comin' home to see my ma."

"Didn't he send me a message?"

"Yeah, well, in a way. He don't want to see you dead, that's for certain, Marshal."

"Neither do I."

"Yeah, don't we all? Bart only wants a truce for one day. He does want to ride in and see his ma, and ride out. That's fair enough, don't you think?"

"It's not a decision I can make."

"Why not? You're the great Marshal Will Titus who can do nothing wrong. Who'd ever call you?"

"I would."

"I'm told that Bart's having a hard time holding his men back. They want to ride in and salivate you, Marshal."

"Gorila tried it, among others. They're chained up over there and there's plenty of chain left." He looked directly at Bowman. "For those that survive, that is."

"Bart's really worried about you, Marshal."

"I hope that's the worst worry that'll ever assail him."

"Your answer is no, I take it?"

"You take it right."

Young Bowman shrugged. "Well, that's your tough luck. Now, you excuse me, I gotta ride by and see my ma. So long, Marshal Titus."

Titus nodded and watched Bowman mount and ride north. The dust of his departure still hung in the air when Doctor McNair pulled his buggy horse to a stop in front of where Titus sat on the porch. Doc pulled a weight from the floor of the buggy and snapped the anchoring line to Nellie's bit and dropped the weight on the ground. The horse tested it as McNair came toward Titus. He had discarded the bandage around his head and wore his usual soft dark hat.

"Hello, Will. Wasn't that Brace Bowman just left here?"

"It was."

"What'd he want?"

"Same thing everybody wants. For me to clear out and leave Bart Laney alone."

McNair sat on the edge of the porch, closing his eyes for a moment. He opened his eyes and looked at Titus. "Don't you feel the trap closing in on you, Will?"

Titus was not a worrying man but he gave a moment's thought to McNair's question and chose not to answer. "How's your head?"

"My head's all right. A little rap with a pistol barrel."

"Who done it?"

"Besides Gorila, there was a Jack and a Ben and a Sam. Don't know their last names."

"Jack Lickey, a shooter of some repute and one of Bart's gang. Ben Timmons and Sam Agnew, all of them wanted of course."

"How in the world do you keep up with all these outlaws?"

"A good lawman knows as much about outlaws, maybe more, than they know about themselves."

"Did you ever put yourself in Bart Laney's boots?"

"Many a time. I know you got too many people to take care of to sit here jawing with me, Doc. What're you here for?"

"I just returned from patching up a few men at Gentility," McNair said unhappily. "A great many unprincipled men are gathering there, Marshal, and their number increases day by day. They want both you and Bart."

"Both of us?"

McNair nodded. "Bart for the reward money. It's quite a sum."

"And me?"

McNair smiled. "You're a thorn in the side of every outlaw between the Mississippi and the high Sierras. There would be a big celebration among the criminal element if the celebrated Marshal Will Titus was six feet under."

"There'd be another to take my place."

"A Will Titus comes along once in a century. Have you thought of retirement, Will?"

"No, not up to now. I wouldn't know what to do with myself."

"Maybe you'd better think about it. Your right wrist bother you, Will?"

Titus stopped rocking, stiffening. Had he been massaging his wrist? He did it unconsciously at times. "I took a knife cut there last year," Titus said.

"And cut a tendon?"

Titus stared at McNair. "I'd rather not talk about it, Doctor. And I trust you'll not repeat this to anyone."

McNair stood up. "You can trust in that, of course."

He walked out to his buggy horse, unsnapped the tiedown

and dropped it on the floor of the buggy. He climbed in and settled himself, looking at Titus. "Good day, Will," he said, and added wistfully, "Sure wish I'd known Mark Twain was here. I'd have been delighted to meet him in person."

"He left in a big hurry," Titus said and waved a farewell, resisting an impulse to tell Doc that it wasn't Mark Twain at all.

Bishop Adam Cantrell stood at his back corral with one boot resting on the bottom rail, staring at two horses within the enclosure. The two horses had belonged to Bogan and Kile, one of whom was dead, the other chained to Bowman's snubbing post. The horses were gaunted but basically outstanding animals. The bishop, hearing footsteps, took his foot from the rail and turned, watching Grafton and Lucian Bowman approach.

The two men stopped beside Cantrell, both of them looking at the two horses, with some envy. The bishopric was entitled to windfalls such as these.

"Mighty poor," Grafton said.

"Both of them sorefooted," Bowman added.

"The men who ride the high country are hard on horses," Cantrell said. "These two will be fine after a spell of regular feeding. Don't need shoeing just yet, Lucian."

Grafton and Bowman nodded agreement.

They were silent for a long period and then Bishop Cantrell cleared his throat. "What we need to discuss had better not be talked about in God's house."

"It's all right with me," the blacksmith said, flexing his muscular arms. He added as an afterthought, "Brace come home a while back. He told me Bart is at their camp."

"We're not quite ready," Cantrell said nervously. "I've talked to Titus without satisfaction. And I've not heard from President Cleveland."

"I don't believe you'll hear from him, Bishop," Grafton offered. "As far as he's concerned, we're beyond the pale. We've no rights, none at all. We learned that a long, long time ago."

"I'm inclined to agree with Brother Grafton," Bowman said. Cantrell looked from one to the other. "You may be right. I'll give the President two more days and then we'll act. It'll take at least two days to get the men we want."

Bowman flexed his mighty hands. "I'm not goin' ag'in you, Bishop," he said, "but I truly believe we'd be better off to leave the Danites out of this. We'll profit by keeping this problem right here in our own valley."

"You got a plan, Lucian?" the bishop's voice held a note of aggravation.

"It's simple. Bart can get to the Gentile's sheep wagon—"

"The sheep wagon belongs to me," Cantrell said.

"Yes, of course. Bart can get here just fine. The trouble lies between here and his home, in the person of Marshal Will Titus. The man never sleeps that I can tell."

"He sleeps all right," Grafton said, "but like a cat. One movement and he's awake and alert. And he sleeps in a different place every night, on the ground. At times I think Satan possesses him."

"The devil is in him all right," Cantrell said thoughtfully. "But, get on, Lucian. I'm not anxious for more killing."

"We'll fix a possum belly on the stone wagon," Lucian said. "A couple of steer hides or a tarp hanging under the wagon bed. Bart can hide in the possum belly and the wagon can be pulled into my shop for repairs. Then, in the dead of night, Bart can transfer from the possum belly to the coffin. We'll worry about getting him out of the house later."

"One thing about Titus, he misses nothing," Grafton interposed. "He'll spot that possum belly in a minute. We've never had one on the stone wagon."

"We'll put the possum belly on right now," Lucian said. "And let him get used to it. We should have one anyway, to pick up firewood for the meetin' house. We should have started using it long ago."

"It might work," Cantrell said. "Let us pray on it and get some guidance from the Lord."

CHAPTER 12

Jenny Gardner, like everyone else in Circle City, came to the door when war whoops and Texas yells broke the quiet of the town.

"Whatever in this world!"

Titus inclined his head but did not respond. He watched a strange sight for Circle City, or any other spot on the globe.

The man on the loping white horse waved his hat, his long hair flowing in the wind. He was dressed in white buckskin with fringe all around, as were the white gauntlets, military type. He packed two pearl-handled .45's in elaborate tooled leather holsters, attached to an even more elaborate belt.

Behind him on a dead run came a Deadwood stage, with driver and shotgun guard whooping and hollering up a storm.

Behind this stage, six Sioux braves in full war paint and feathers emitted war whoops as their ponies galloped full tilt, the braves waving spears.

This entourage came to an abrupt halt before Grafton's house while all the able-bodied citizens of Circle City stared in amazement.

The man dismounted from the prancing white horse. A man in cowboy regalia leaped from the stage and ran to take the reins of the white horse.

Titus thought: Buffalo Bill Cody, by god!

Cody brushed his gauntleted hands over his immaculate sleeves and sauntered toward Titus.

As Cody walked toward Titus he removed his gloves in theatrical slow motion, walking grandly.

"Good day to you, sir!" Cody said heartily, extending a

bared hand. His mustache and beard, well-kept, well-trimmed, gleamed in the sunlight. "I'm Colonel William F. Cody—Buffalo Bill, that is—and I'm here to offer you a job."

Titus rose to his feet to shake hands with the famous scout and showman, feeling no sign of calluses on Cody's hand. He thought: By god, he hasn't worked for some time.

"Pleased," Titus said. "I've got a job."

"As the world is well aware," Cody said in that hearty manner. "I just completed a tour around the country. I want to put together a bigger and better show and take it to England for the Queen's Golden Jubilee."

"Sorry, Mr. Cody. Like I said, I have a job."

"Where you could easily get yourself killed," Cody said.

"That could happen anywhere, anytime."

"Less likely in a Wild West show. I haven't lost a man yet."

"Sorry, Mr. Cody. I'm not cut out to be an actor." Titus looked at the Indians. "I don't see Sitting Bull," he said.

"Well, you know he did work for me. I paid him fifty dollars a week. But the Bull felt like a great chief such as he is shouldn't be on display like that."

"He'd be a hit in England. Why don't you ask him to go? I understand he has a great admiration for Queen Victoria."

"Well, to tell the truth I did ask him to go. He turned me down, Marshal. Said his people needed him in these times. Government trying to grab more of their land, and all that."

"That makes sense. And you paid the Bull fifty dollars a week? That's quite a bit of money, Mr. Cody."

"You betcha."

"How about those warriors? Do you pay them that much?"

"Well, no, but then they're warriors. Sitting Bull is probably the most famous chief among all the Indians."

Cody seated himself on the edge of the porch, pushed his hat back and surveyed the distant mountains. "By god, I miss the great outdoors, the plains and mountains, indeed I do. The real life out here, that's what it is, Marshal. The freedom. That's what I value most of all." He sighed a deep sigh. "It preys on my mind continually, to chuck it all and go back to scouting and fighting Indians."

Titus didn't point out that the Indian wars were over and most of the tribes on reservations, closely guarded by the Army. "And give up all this?" Titus asked, waving his hand at the stage coach and the braves quietly sitting their ponies.

"Soft living has its points. Yes, and I—" He broke off, staring up the road.

Titus, though unruffled by Cody's appearance, had not maintained his usual alert watch. Therefore, Thomas P. Riley was within pistol shot before Titus detected him, and then only by Cody's reaction.

Riley came swinging steadily toward Titus, ignoring the Indians, the cowboys and stage coach. He carried an old cap and ball pistol, thrust forward at the ready.

"You're done for, Titus," Riley shouted. "You've spoiled our town, killed our people . . . my two sons . . ."

"What the hell!" Buffalo Bill said, rising to his feet and stepping up on the porch as though nearness to Titus provided him with some protection.

"Stay put," Titus ordered and stepped to the ground. To Riley he said, "You're all wrong, Constable. You'd better go home and let your good sense get a chance to work."

The answer came in a puff of smoke from the old pistol in Riley's hands. The bullet passed through the back of the rocking chair and lodged in the wall of Grafton's house.

Buffalo Bill dove headlong from the porch to the ground and crawled rapidly out of sight. His white fringed gauntlets lay on the porch, abandoned in their owner's hasty departure.

Riley fired again and the bullet whispered by Titus' cheek, went through the open door and shattered a picture on the wall of Grafton's parlor.

Still Titus did not draw his weapon. He stood upright, his legs spread, fighting a battle that was new to him. In all his years of experience he'd never hesitated to draw his gun and shoot to kill.

Riley now dropped to one knee and aimed carefully, one eye closed.

The cowboy holding Cody's white horse pulled his pistol and fired one round into Riley's back, the bullet piercing Riley's heart. Riley fell forward and the toes of his boots kicked up a little plume of dust. After that slight twitch of his body, Riley remained still.

Lucian Bowman, his leather apron flapping, ran across the road and knelt beside Riley. After feeling for Riley's pulse, and finding none, Lucian raised his head and looked at Titus.

"Great God Almighty," he said, lifting his eyes to the sky. He made no sound after those words but his lips moved. Then he rose to his feet, staring fixedly at Titus.

"Will, Will," he said despairingly, and leaned down and scooped up Riley effortlessly and turned and strode down the road.

The crowd that had scattered as Riley fired his shots regrouped and stood staring in morbid fascination at Titus.

"Move along, folks," Titus said. "There's been enough of a disturbance for one day."

Cody came around the corner dusting off his immaculate white buckskin shirt which had been dirtied. He said, "Marshal, that was a close call. If my man hadn't been alert I'm afraid that fellow would have got you."

The crowd dispersed slowly, reluctantly, until the street was emptied of all but three young boys. Titus motioned with both hands and they fled toward Grafton's store. "You may be right," Titus said. "He had dead aim on me." He felt an emptiness that was unfamiliar.

"Well, you're a cool one," Cody said. "I wish I could talk you into joining my show."

"Why don't you get Wild Bill Hickok?"

"Uh, well, Bill did work for me but he didn't pan out."

"Why not, he seems to be a pretty colorful sort?"

"Well, I had him in this little scene, where he was sitting

around a campfire with a bunch of men, scouts that is, drinking whiskey and telling tall stories."

"That appears to be an easy enough job."

"Yeah, well, they didn't really drink whiskey, not real whiskey. The drink was tea and at first taste Wild Bill spat it out and cursed everybody roundly. He quit the show shortly thereafter."

"I'm sorry it didn't work out," Titus said. "But my job is here and here I'll stay 'til it's finished."

"You're a man of iron, Marshal. I can see I can't persuade you and all I can say is good luck to you and good-bye."

"Thanks," Titus said and watched Cody retrieve his gloves from the front porch and draw them on with a flourish. He touched his hat brim to Titus and strode, with a showmanlike walk, to his white horse.

Taking the reins from the cowboy he mounted as though performing for an audience. The well-trained white horse stood on its hind legs, pawing the air with flailing front hooves while walking a circle, with Cody waving his white hat.

Cody let out a yell and headed north. The stage and six Sioux braves followed. In a short time the entourage disappeared and nothing was left but a dust cloud hanging over the road.

Jenny Gardner emerged from the house, wiping her eyes on her apron. "Poor Brother Riley," she said. "He was such an inoffensive little man. I wonder who'll keep the pigs out our main road now?"

"I'm sorry about Riley."

"The least you could do was arrest the man that shot poor Brother Riley in the back."

"It slipped my mind," Titus said dryly, "seeing as how that shot likely saved my life. Any damage to the house?"

"Brother Grafton's picture of Brother Brigham has been ruined."

"He'll probably find another," Titus said, resuming his seat in the rocking chair.

"Did he—Buffalo Bill, offer you a job?"

"Yes."

"In a Wild West show! He wanted you in his show? That was Buffalo Bill, wasn't he, the one all in white?"

"He said he was. And he looks like pictures I've seen of him. So my guess is that it was Buffalo Bill."

"And he wanted you, he offered you a job!"

"If some of these hooligans who're collecting around here decide to relieve him of his valuables he might not have a Wild West show."

"I presume you'd not go to his rescue if he was accosted?"

"You presume correctly. I'm here for a special purpose."

"God forbid that you'll see it come to pass," Jenny said before disappearing into the house.

It was near dusk when Elizabeth came out of the house across the street. Bats were beginning to come out on their nocturnal flights. She approached in silence and sat on the edge of the porch. "I saw it all, Will and I'm more disturbed than ever. You're not the same man you were when you rode in."

Titus was silent, sitting there flexing his right hand, thinking that she'd hit on something important which he had missed.

"You'd have let yourself be killed before defending yourself. That's the difference."

"You may be right." He waited for a long moment and added, "And then again you may not be."

She twisted her body and looked up at him. "Will, I've worked fixing up the room you and Bart once used. There's no sense you sleeping like some wild animal on the ground or in the brush. You'd be a lot more comfortable over there."

"What's easiest for me may not be the best for what I've got to do."

She turned and got to her knees in front of him and clasped his legs with her arm. "Oh, Will, please, please, don't let this go on any longer!"

He stood up with a sense of shame and deep embarrassment.

Her hands had fallen away when he rose and now he leaned down and lifted her to her feet. "Don't do that, not ever again," he said huskily.

She was babbling almost incoherently: "Things will change, they must change. Ellie Bay is so sure Bart will die he's thinking of taking over now. That means more bloodletting and violence. Ellie will move in, free your prisoners, and kill you, no matter if he loses two or three men."

"You don't know what you're talking about."

"I do, I do." She tried to shake him but couldn't budge his big body. She pressed close to him, her arms around his neck, pulling his head down, her lips seeking his.

He avoided her lips, pulling her arms loose. "I'm not inhuman," he said hoarsely. "Don't do this, Elizabeth."

"I'm trying to save you," she whispered fiercely. "It's not worth it, you'll be sorry for the rest of your life. My mother, she nursed you, Will, you and Bart. You were a greedy baby, Will, maybe that's why you're bigger than Bart—"

"Hush, woman."

"I will not hush—" She stopped speaking at the sound of footsteps out in the darkness. She felt him stiffen as they stepped apart. Grafton warily approached the steps and mounted them, with a "Good evenin', Elizabeth, Marshal," and went on into the house.

Wordlessly, Elizabeth backed away from Titus, turned and descended the steps to walk slowly across the road. Titus could not see her in the darkness but he heard her door open and close.

Hundreds of miles to the east as the crow flies Kid Ringbolt arrived with a Texas herd, ending his first cattle drive at Abilene. While on the trail he had decided definitely it would be his last. He was thoroughly cured of any desire to herd cattle up the long trail again.

Over the boring weeks on the drive he'd heard a thousand stories about the evils of Abilene, stories that had intrigued him somewhat. Of more interest were the stories about the fabled gunfighters who maintained law and order in the whoop-up town of Abilene.

Kid owned an old cap and ball pistol and every chance he got, when he was unobserved, he practiced drawing the gun and pulling the trigger. He believed himself to be pretty handy with that old cap and ball.

As soon as the herd had been shooed into the railroad loading pens he cleaned up and headed for the bright spots, hoping to glimpse one of the famed lawmen.

Just outside the Long Branch, a uniformed law officer was holding a belligerent cowboy against the wall, trying to talk some sense into him.

The cowpuncher's buddy stood unsteadily in the street, wobbly drunk, shouting obscenities at the lawman. The cowboy in the street pulled his pistol as Ringbolt watched, cocked it and unsteadily pointed it at the lawman's back.

Kid Ringbolt yelled louder than he'd ever yelled at a straying cow and pulled his own pistol and fired.

The cowboy with the pistol dropped in his tracks.

What followed happened faster than Ringbolt could keep account of in his excited state. The next thing he knew the cowboy struggling with the lawman was lying in the street with his head bleeding. Men ran back and forth shouting to one another. Kid Ringbolt dazedly watched it all, wondering what the hell had happened.

A half hour later he was seated in the office of the sheriff, a handsome devil who stared at him in some amusement.

"I'm Bat Masterson," the sheriff said. "This here's my brother, Ed, who's chief of police."

Ed was the one Kid Ringbolt had saved from being shot in the back.

Kid Ringbolt's throat grew taut and his mouth dried out and he felt like urinating. "Gl—glad to meetcha," he chattered.

"What's your name, son?" Ed asked in a kindly voice.

"Kid Ringbolt. I just come up the trail and I ain't never goin' back, not by a dang sight."

"Thanks, Kid," Ed Masterson said. "No doubt about it you saved my life."

"Why ain't you goin' back to Texas, son?" Bat asked. "You had your fun yet?"

"I don't drink," Ringbolt said. "I just want to be a lawman. Like you and your brother and some of the others."

"You gotta get some experience," Bat said. "You gotta make your mark. Then the towns come lookin' for you to keep the peace. That's how it works."

"You better go home, son," Ed said quietly. "Lawin' ain't what it's cracked up to be."

"A hell of a lot of fun," Bat said cheerfully.

Ringbolt's chest swelled with pride. Here he was, not quite nineteen years old and talking to two of the famous gunfighters who had turned to lawing. He thought exultantly: wait'll I tell the folks back home. Then he remembered he wouldn't be going back home.

"I'd like to learn how to keep the peace," Ringbolt said. "I want to know how it's done. Then, maybe I can get a job like you two."

"I shot the sheriff," Bat said. "That's how I got my job."

"Stop joshing him, Bat," Ed said. To Ringbolt he said: "Time is running out for our like." Ed was a man well-loved by the citizens of Abilene because of his reluctance to use a gun. He'd rather talk a potential lawbreaker out of trouble rather than pistol whipping him or shooting him down. "By the time you get enough experience to be a lawman, like us, that is, there won't be any demand for your services."

"By god, Ed, I hope you're wrong," Bat said.

"I want to be a lawman," Ringbolt said doggedly.

Ed sighed, a sad sound in the cluttered office. "Well, I owe you something. I can't give you a job but I can give you something." He got up from his chair and went to the desk where Bat was sitting.

Ed opened a desk drawer, pushing Bat's knee out of the way, and took out a pistol and examined it. He spun the cylinder and sighted down the barrel.

"This gun belonged to a feller no longer in the land o' the living. It's a .44 Colt, what they call a Peacemaker, and fairly new. That cap and ball hogleg you're carryin' is not a fit weapon for a lawman."

Ringbolt's heart was beating wildly as he accepted the pistol with trembling hands. He looked at it with awe and then pulled out the cap and ball and pushed his new weapon into the old holster.

"Mister Bat, Mister Ed, I ain't never goin' to forget this moment. Not ever."

"Just one thing," Ed said in a warning voice. "Don't let that piece get you into trouble, Kid."

Bat laughed, "It'll get you in trouble if you don't learn to unload it in a hurry. When somebody's tryin' to unload his'n at you."

Ringbolt nodded gravely. He handed the cap and ball to Ed. "I reckon I won't be needin' it no more." He looked at Ed and then at Bat, both of whom regarded him without a hint of humor, almost as if he were really one of them.

He admired Bat the most because he was not solemn like Ed. Ringbolt determined to pattern himself after Bat who appeared more formidable than Ed. "I reckon I better git movin'," he said. "Thanky, thanks a heap, both o' you."

"Well, you're entirely welcome," Ed said. "Where you headin' out to, son?"

"Think I'll drift west a piece," Ringbolt said, and lounged through the door like he'd seen others do it.

Ringbolt had heard the talk about Will Titus, the famous marshal, and the outlaw, Bart Laney, and the coming big showdown. If he, Kid Ringbolt, could down Laney he'd have instant success. The thought of facing Laney in a gun fight set his blood racing. He'd have time along the way to practice a fast draw. By the time he reached Circle City he'd be the fastest gun anywhere around.

Ringbolt mounted his cow pony and turned the animal toward the setting sun. He figured it'd take him a couple of weeks to reach Circle City. There was a mighty big mountain up there, waiting for him. He'd never seen the Rockies but he'd heard about them.

CHAPTER 13

Jenny Gardner stood defiantly between Titus and the three women standing resolutely at the edge of Grafton's front yard.

"It's Marshal Titus we want to talk to, Jenny Gardner," the spokeswoman said stridently.

"Jenny, go inside," Titus ordered, irritation in his voice. He'd not had much experience with quarreling women.

Jenny turned and looked at him, her lips pursed. She held a mixing bowl and spoon against her aproned stomach. She silently marched to the front door, snatched it open and disappeared inside, slamming the door with unnecessary force.

Titus rose leisurely from the rocker, removed his hat and sauntered to the top step. "Sorry I can't offer you all a seat," he said. "There's only one."

"We didn't come to sit," said one of Cantrell's wives. She was a thin, gaunt woman with lackluster hair drawn severely back into an untidy bun at the nape of her neck.

Titus thought: God'll surely reward Cantrell for marrying this one for no man in his right mind would have her. Aloud, he said, "What can I do for you ladies?"

"Those men out there you've got chained up. It's inhuman. That's no way to treat the Lord's children."

Her two companions nodded agreement.

"They're not the Lord's children," Titus said. "They'd cut your throat for a chew of tobacco."

"There's good in the worst of them."

"I doubt it. But I've little choice. Circle City has no jail house. There are no civic-minded citizens who'll give me or rent me a secure place for these desperate men."

"What about their bodily needs?"

"Well, that is a problem. I throw them a few scraps and carry a bucket of water once or twice a day. They're not active so they don't need much."

"It's not Christianlike," Mrs. Cantrell said.

"I make no claim to divinity but I do recognize the problem. The U. S. Government will make a reasonable payment to your Ladies Aid or whatever it's called, for the feeding and care of these damnable outlaws."

"How much would the U. S. Government be willing to pay?" Mrs. Cantrell asked, while her two companions leaned forward, listening intently and with some avarice.

Titus had decided that she was at least wife number two or possibly number three. "Two dollars a day per man."

The three women put their heads together and talked in whispers, glancing slyly at Titus now and then. Mrs. Cantrell turned back to Titus. "That seems quite generous," she said. "We'll have to consult the bishopric before we can decide."

"Go on, Melissa," one of the women muttered. "Tell him the other."

Melissa Cantrell flushed, her thin lips growing even thinner and then puckering. She straightened her bony shoulders and cleared her throat. "There ought to be a screen put up so they aren't in plain sight when they—when they—when they you know what."

"I had them dig a hole," Titus observed. "It's lined with lime—"

"They're in plain view during daylight when they do their business," Mrs. Cantrell blazed. "And they always wait until a lady is passing when they do it. It's a disgrace, that's what it is!"

"I'll attend to it," Titus said resignedly.

"Thank you, Marshal," Mrs. Cantrell said stiffly. The three of them looked at one another in triumph. They turned as one and marched to the path that ran alongside the road, trudging north in militant single file, Mrs. Cantrell leading.

Jenny raised a cloud of dust sweeping off Grafton's front porch. She moved the broom methodically, sweeping in one direction, toward the edge of the porch, moving the sand and dust a section at a time. Eventually she came to Marshal Titus' rocking chair.

"You want me to move?"

She rested her two hands on top of the broom, looking at him with a puzzled frown. "I'll sweep around you, so just sit there."

He looked at the broom instead of meeting her gaze, wondering at the strange feelings she engendered in him. She brought him back to a time when the world was a better place. Stranger still, she aroused a yearning tenderness for her that he found unsettling, almost as much so as his desire to protect her. Protect her from what? he wondered.

"You're not safe on this porch, Marshal."

He stifled a curse. "It's a risk I'll have to take."

"It's all so senseless. What's one outlaw more or less?"

"I'm bound by oath of office to apprehend law breakers."

"After seeing some of these deputy marshals chasing after polygamists, I'd say some lawmen are bad as the outlaws, if not worse."

"That's not my concern at this time."

"What is your concern, Marshal?"

"I told you. To apprehend people who break the law."

"Go down to Gentility and clean it up," she said. "You could arrest anyone you come on and chances are great he'd be a criminal."

"I may go through there when I leave here—if I'm not encumbered with prisoners."

She made an impatient motion with her broom. "Have you considered that you may be seeking revenge rather than upholding the law? I don't know much about it but there's dark rumors about your hatred for these people."

His cold glance frightened her and she tightened her grip on the broom handle as though preparing to defend herself. With relief she watched the wrath fade from his eyes and face as he resumed his slow studied motion of the rocking chair. She edged toward the door.

"You haven't finished sweeping the porch," he reminded her.

She gave him a withering stare and swept inside, slamming the door shut with a bang.

He sighed and settled back in his rocker only to rise and stare at two approaching horsemen. He waited, watching, as they stopped their horses before the house. Titus reached for his shotgun. One of the riders held a small boy on the saddle before him and now he lifted the child and leaned down and placed him on the ground and dismounted. The other man remained in the saddle. "No need for the Greener, Marshal," said the man on the ground. "We're deputy U.S. marshals out of Carson City."

Titus stared at them without acknowledging the introduction. The more they come the worse they get, he thought.

"We're over here chasin' polygamists," the man continued. "This young feller here is gonna show us one with at least a dozen wives. That so, sonny?"

The child nodded solemnly.

The second man now dismounted and both of them tied their horses to a poplar tree beside the road. "This is the place, ain't it, sonny?"

"Yes, sir. Right back there." He started toward the rear of the house and the two men loosened their guns and started after the boy.

Titus raised his shotgun. "Just a minute, there," he said. All three of them stopped, staring at Titus.

"I've been here for a spell," Titus said. "I can say for sure there's no one back there answering that description."

"We got ten John Doe warrants, Marshal Titus," the man in the lead said. "We get a hundred a piece for them. All we gotta do is identify a known polygamist and this young fella says he can show us one. Now, just lower that shotgun and we'll see what we'll see."

"See for yourself," Titus said indifferently but did not lower the shotgun. He motioned with it. "Get on with it and find out for yourself and then clear out."

"You might find yourself in need of our help."

"I doubt it. Get on with it." Titus watched them step gingerly toward the rear of the house. Both marshals drew their pistols.

Titus stepped to the ground and followed a respectable distance behind. He stopped at the corner of the house in order to keep the Laney house in sight. Peso, his horse, was chewing on the neck of Grafton's buggy horse.

The boy leading the two marshals pointed to the chicken yard. In the enclosure a dozen hens and a rooster scratched in the dirt.

One of the marshals reached down and grabbed the boy by the shoulder and shook him so violently the boy's hat fell to the ground.

"Stop shaking that kid," Titus commanded.

The marshal let the boy go and swung around, his face livid. "Damn kid lied to us," he complained. "Said he'd show us a family with one male and ten, twelve females."

"He wasn't lying," Titus said. "Might I suggest you get on your horses and get the hell out of here?"

The two marshals stalked by him, untied their horses and, mounting, rode south toward Gentility.

Grinning, the boy sauntered over beside Titus and watched them disappear around a bend in the road. "Bet they thought sure they'd corraled a polygamist."

"You run along, boy," Titus said sternly. "And don't go misleading the law, not ever again, hear?"

"Yes, sir, Marshal," the boy said meekly and scooted away. He cast one look over his shoulder and was grinning widely.

From his vantage point on Grafton's front porch, Titus watched steam drift out of the flue of Lucian Bowman's forge as the blacksmith doused the fire for the day. From out beyond the fruit orchard a crow called hoarsely and was answered by another. The rooster crowed in the backyard chicken pen. A pig rooted in the dry irrigation ditch across the road, grunting contentedly when it found a tidbit.

Titus straightened and stopped rocking to stare at an approaching rig, coming from the north. The vehicle, pulled by two sturdy gray horses, appeared to be a doughtery wagon. The driver, a slight man with a drooping mustache, did not appear to be a military man.

As the driver guided the team off the road and into the area before Bowman's Smithy, Titus read the legend on the side panels that had been added to the doughtery wagon: "Traveling Photographer of The West" and below that a roughly painted mountain with a white tip simulating snow.

The driver wound his reins around a whip socket and stepped to the wheel and then jumped to the ground as Bowman strode forward to meet him.

Titus touched his underarm pistol and grabbing his Winchester stepped to the ground and strode rapidly across the road to stand silently behind the new arrival. Bowman looked at him across the man's shoulder but made no indication of his presence.

"Hello. You Mr. Bowman?" the newcomer asked.

Lucian nodded.

The man extended his hand. "I'm Manfred Pierpont, photographer," he said. "One of my horses needs shoeing."

"I shoe horses. But I've put out my fire for the day."

"Oh, I'm in no big hurry. What's the charge for the job? Just one shoe. The right front of the gray on this side."

"Six bits," Lucian said.

"Seems reasonable. Say, what're those fellows chained up for?"

The prisoners had crawled to their feet and stood looking at

Pierpont, not saying anything but poking each other with their elbows and grinning.

"Ask the marshal," Lucian said. "He's standing right behind you."

The photographer whirled, a startled look on his face. He put his thumbs in his galluses and snapped them, his brown eyes turning anxious. "Well, I declare! You're the famous Marshal Titus, I take it?"

"Hey, Mister Picture Man, wanna take our pichur?" Shagrun called.

"Don't pay them any mind," Titus said. "They're criminals awaiting transport to jail."

"A trip you'll never take, Marshal," Shagrun said viciously, not smiling now. "Not with us nohow."

"Shut up and sit down, Shagrun," Titus said, "and the rest of you, too."

The prisoners slowly obeyed, shaking their chains unnecessarily.

Pierpont cleared his throat. "I just pulled in to get my horse shod—"

"I heard," Titus said.

"Well, Mr. Bowman can't do the job today. I'll just camp right here until he lights his fire in the morning."

"No, you can't do that," Titus said. "Too near these vermin."

Pierpont snapped his galluses. "Well, what'll I do? I can't drive that horse much longer, hoof wore down to the quick almost. I—"

"You might try Elizabeth Laney," Bowman said. "Family next door. They own the fruit orchard. Probably let you camp there in the orchard."

"That all right with you, Marshal?" Pierpont asked worriedly.

Titus shrugged and shifted his Winchester to his left hand. "That's your lookout. What're you doing in these parts?"

"You, Marshal. I come down to take some pictures. The

newspapers and magazines back east are wild for pictures of what's taking place out here."

Titus grunted. "I've no time for pictures," he snapped. "You're in danger, Pierpont, and the closer you get to me the more dangerous it is." He wheeled and went back to his watching post, keeping an eye on Bowman and Pierpont but not neglecting his now habitual sweep of all the terrain.

He watched Bowman and Pierpont talking, with Lucian gesturing toward the Laney house. The photographer nodded to Bowman, wheeled and walked to the gate of the Laney house, opened it and walked on to the porch where he knocked on the door. Elizabeth opened the door to him and stood there talking, with the photographer gesturing toward the smithy, toward Titus and finally to the fruit orchard. Elizabeth shook her head, nodded once and twice and money exchanged hands. The photographer returned to the smithy, climbed up to the wagon seat, unwound the reins and drove out, circling to dip down into the irrigation ditch and up into the fruit orchard. He got down from the wagon and began unharnessing his team.

Watching, Titus wondered if Pierpont had been sent by Bart. He considered the matter calmly, from all angles. He called up in his mind all he knew about Bart, plus all the gossip, rumors and outright lies he'd heard repeatedly over the years. There was nothing to indicate that Bart Laney would resort to finagling a pretended photographer into Circle City, for the purpose of getting past Will Titus.

No, he concluded, when and if Bart Laney came to his mother's house in Circle City, he'd come alone and openly. That was Bart Laney's way, from all that he, Will Titus, knew of the man.

That doesn't mean, he cautioned himself, that he'd not keep a close eye on Pierpont. The man might have designs of his own, namely the ten thousand dollars on Laney's head.

More than one man had been tempted by a lot less. Yes, he thought, Pierpont will bear watching.

Kid Ringbolt lost all track of time on his westward ride to
Circle City and possible fame and fortune. A dozen or more
times at various parts of the day he had stopped his horse to
gaze into the vast distances ahead, debating whether to continue on. Deadening his mind to the unknown lying ahead, he
pushed on doggedly, following the rails at first, relishing the
moment of excitement when a passenger or freight train
chugged past, waving his hat. The engineers sometimes responded with a languid upflung hand. The passengers waved
briskly. The freight train crews ignored him. Always, after the
train passed the land seemed more silent, and lonelier than
ever. He spent an inordinate amount of time rationalizing himself to his pony, Slam Bang.

After leaving the railroad near Fort Bridger and riding into
the wilds of the Uintas, he fell victim to rigors of the trail time
after time. His coffee gone, his flour ruined in a turbulent river
crossing, he was reduced to eating what he could find along
the way. "No wonder them pore damn Indians look so pore,"
he confided to Slam Bang.

Finally, Slam Bang threw a shoe but Ringbolt didn't notice
its loss until the shoe was somewhere behind him and he
wasn't about to go back looking for it. He walked, leading
Slam Bang, hunger gnawing at his guts like a hungry coyote.

He pushed on, though, his initial dream now an obsession.
He encountered a remote homesteader on the Green River,
south of the Ouray Indian Reservation.

The snug, one-room, sod-roofed log cabin, with a window
having real glass, was a welcome sight to Ringbolt. He had
started thinking he was the only human left in the world. He
led Slam Bang toward the cabin, past a small field of grain,
and Slam Bang seemed to pick up a little spirit.

A buxom woman followed by two children came from the
cabin and watched his approach. He got within hollering distance and started shouting and she shouted back. When he got
up close he felt like he was acquainted with her. He lifted his
hat. "Howdy, ma'am, whereabouts am I?"

Smiling shyly, she said, "This is Hanchey's place. I'm Mrs. Hanchey. We're about a hundred fifty miles from Salt Lake City, that way." She pointed to the northwest. The two children, a boy with freckles, and a girl in braids, clung to their mother's skirts and stared owlishly at Ringbolt.

"Nice place you got here. I'm Kid, er, I mean Clarence Ringbolt."

She beamed proudly. "Mr. Hanchey will be along soon. He's plowin' out south of here. Can I get you a drink of water?"

"I'd sure appreciate that, ma'am," Ringbolt said, thinking that he'd much rather have something from what was being cooked inside the cabin. The smell was overpowering and caused him to feel faint, to salivate, and his innards growled.

She brought a gourd dipper, dripping, and offered it to him. He drank deeply and said, "I'd ought to take care of my horse. Ol' Slam Bang's just about done in." He gave her the dipper.

"Waterin' trough's in back," she said. "Help yourself. And give him some hay from the shed."

"Ma'am, I'm powerful grateful." Ringbolt nodded and led his horse around the cabin. The little boy followed him, watching his every move.

He let the horse drink. He brought a fork or two of hay. He examined the splintered hoof, sighing with frustration.

"Pa'll shoe your horse," the boy offered. "He kin do anythin', Pa kin."

"I'll bet he can," Ringbolt said absently. A corral in back held two milch cows and a very fine looking gray horse that threw up its head and neighed as Ringbolt let Slam Bang's hoof back to the ground. A fat sow with five piglets rooted inside the corral. A flock of chickens scratched and pecked oblivious to the horse.

The little boy grinned. He had a front tooth missing and a smudge of dirt on his cheek. Ringbolt saw the expression on the boy's face change and he glanced over his shoulder. A bearded man was leading the horse toward the corral gate.

The little boy screamed, "Ma, somebody's stealin' ol' Gray."
He ran toward the corral shouting and waving his arms. The
horse thief ignored him as he slipped a bridle over Gray's nose
and swung up bareback. The woman came around the corner
of the cabin, shouting and waving her apron.

The horse thief clapped his heels to Gray's sides and the big
horse lunged through the open gate. Ringbolt drew his pistol.
"Hold up there!" he shouted and leveled the pistol.

The horse thief jerked out his gun as Gray thundered away,
and fired at Ringbolt. The bullet knocked his left leg out from
under him and he fell backward. Raising on one elbow, he
fired. The horse thief sailed off the horse, landed with a thump,
bounced a little and lay still. Gray circled, reins dangling,
neighing uneasily. Slam Bang pranced around the pile of hay
but didn't stop eating.

The little boy ran out and gathered up Gray's reins and led
him to the corral. Mrs. Hanchey come running up to Ringbolt
and knelt beside him, her face distraught. "You hurt?" she
asked worriedly, as Ringbolt sat up and ejected a spent shell
from his pistol. He reloaded it and holstered the gun. His boot
had filled with blood and felt squishy. "Dang near ruined my
only pair o' boots," he muttered.

Mrs. Hanchey laughed hysterically and then attempted to
remove his boot. She tugged and tugged, and then said, "Let's
get you up to the house."

She helped him up and he limped beside her toward the
house. She had him sit on the ground while she told the little
girl, "Ruthie, go fetch the bearskin rug."

The little girl ran inside the cabin and came out with a
bearskin which Mrs. Hanchey spread on the ground. She made
him move to the rug.

"Ain't nothin' but a scratch," he protested.

She finally worried the boot off. Ringbolt had long since
worn out his socks and his foot was so grimy he blushed and
tried to hide it.

She pushed his pants leg up and bared the ugly, gaping hole

in his leg. Just looking at it made him feel faint. The bullet had
entered the leg halfway between ankle and knee, apparently
touched the bone and glanced off, tearing the big muscle in
the back of his leg. She shook the boot and the bullet fell out
on the ground.

"Ezra, fetch the turps," she told the little boy. To Ringbolt,
she said, "Turpentine is all we have. But it'll keep it from fes-
terin', I'm hopin'."

Ringbolt gasped with pain when she poured turpentine over
the wound. She clucked sympathetically and said, "It hurts
now but it'll save a lot of misery later on."

"I'll take your word for it," he said, gritting his teeth.

She gave him a tin cup of warm, bitter-tasting liquid that
she assured him would help heal. "It's herb tea," she said, "the
Indians swear by it."

Afterward, he dozed, to be awakened later by the jangle of
trace chains and the sound of voices. He opened his eyes to see
a tall, bearded man staring down at him. The man held the
reins of two heavy plow horses. He nodded to Ringbolt. "Sorry
you ran into trouble at my house," he rumbled. "I'm Ezra
Hanchey."

"I'm Ringbolt," Kid mumbled, sitting up. "Kid Ringbolt
from down Texas way."

"You're a long way from home," Ezra said. "Mrs. Hanchey
told me you saved my horse. I thank you."

"Mighty fine horse, too," Ringbolt said.

"One of the best in the whole Territory," Hanchey said. "I'd
have been mighty put out to lose Gray."

"Who—who was the horse thief?"

"Stranger to me. But we're right off what they call the outlaw trail. From Wyoming down to Arizona, they drift back and
forth all the time. Mighty tough, some of them."

Ezra squatted and looked at the wound in Ringbolt's leg.
"Mrs. Hanchey done all that can be done, I reckon." He
looked at the sky. "Be dark soon. We ought to get supper out
of the way before it gets too dark to see."

"It's ready, Mr. Hanchey," the farmer's wife said.

"I'll put the stock away and be right in," Hanchey said, rising and moving away with his two plow horses.

Mrs. Hanchey helped Ringbolt into the cabin and got him seated at the table. He breathed deeply of the big bowl of stew from which steam rose. The evening chill had set in and the cabin felt warm and cozy.

Hanchey came in and closed the door. He seated himself at the head of the table and his wife and children dropped their chins to chest as he intoned a blessing.

Mrs. Hanchey served Ringbolt first, dishing out a generous helping of stew. Hanchey said, "What brings you to this part of the world, Mr. Ringbolt?"

"Well, I'm on my way to Circle City," Ringbolt said, dipping his spoon into the stew and transferring it to his mouth. He grew faint with the taste of good food and tried to keep himself from wolfing it down.

"You're nearly there. You a member of the faith?"

"Huh? What's that?"

"Do you belong to the Brotherhood? The Church."

"No, sir. My folks are all hardshell Baptists. I reckon I'm not much of anything."

"What's your business in Circle City?"

"Well, you see, I'm goin' down there and see if I can't have a showdown with Bart Laney. You see, if I—" He stopped speaking as Hanchey's face grew wrathful. Hanchey rose and leaned across the table and snatched the bowl from before him. His face was stormy as he said, "You'd go down there and gun down Bart Laney? I can't break bread with you, young man. But for Laney we'd never have made it here. He's a good man, the fairest and best I know—"

"Mr. Hanchey, our guest saved Gray," Mrs. Hanchey said. "We can't turn him out like this. He's hurt, too."

"Hush, woman! I'm master in this house and I'll say what is to be and what's not to be."

She dropped her head and sighed into silence.

Hanchey thrust the bowl at Ringbolt and said, "Here, take this outside and finish it. I'll not have you in my house."

"His horse needs shoein', Pa," the little boy piped up. "An' he did save ol' Gray—"

"You had best be quiet," Hanchey warned in a dangerous tone.

"Yes, sir, Pa."

Ringbolt took the bowl of stew and limped outside. What the hell've I got myself into? he wondered.

CHAPTER 14

Chief U.S. Marshal Eldon Flagle, a man of imposing bulk, wearing a narrow-brimmed Stetson, and a walrus mustache, regarded Marshal Titus narrowly and said, "No, I'm not here specifically to parley with you, Marshal. I've other duties in this Territory, such as a personal review of our program against bigamists, of which you have no doubt heard."

Flagle was an anomaly in the ranks of United States marshals, none of which ranked higher than he. Many U.S. marshals, in fact most of them, were politicians of varying degrees of skill. Flagle, while a consummate politician too, was one of the few of his breed with a history behind him of gun and horse and lonely and dangerous duties as a border lawman. Appointed by Abraham Lincoln, succeeding Presidents had seen fit to retain his services in spite of his bluntness.

Titus nodded thoughtfully. "It crossed my mind that you might be calling on me," he said. "The ruling bishopric had advised me that he wrote a complaint to our President regarding my activity here."

Flagle maintained his unsmiling attitude. "My business here perhaps would have been delayed had you not been involved, Marshal. I was counseled by the President prior to my departure from our nation's capital. I must confess that you were the subject of much of that counseling."

"I didn't know the President was aware I am alive," Titus said politely.

"Under ordinary circumstances, perhaps not. These are not ordinary circumstances. Your pursuit of Laney is very much in the news these days, Marshal. It's political, I might add."

"I've orders signed by you," Titus said. "I was directed to apprehend Laney as expeditiously as possible. Did you sign a paper not knowing its contents?"

"Laney has become a national issue. The railroads, you know, are a powerful constituency, as are the banks. They've applied pressure at the highest levels. Naturally, I selected you because I believed you to be possibly the best law enforcement officer in the business. This I know from a knowledge of your record since you became a U.S. marshal. The President appointed you at my behest and the Senate approved his appointment unanimously. I have the utmost confidence in your ability to take Laney."

"Are you now ordering me to cease and desist?"

Flagle cleared his throat uncomfortably. "Ah, Titus, I would prefer you to make that decision."

"On my own initiative?"

"Yes. Yes, on your own."

"Am I to understand that you are backtracking, sir?"

Flagle nodded almost imperceptibly. "That's precisely what I'm doing. It's not my choice."

"There's more here than meets the eye, just one hell of a lot more."

"Good god, Titus, there was a time when you could have taken Laney without all this ruckus and commotion."

"You're referring no doubt to the time when the governor, at the behest of the railroads and banks, offered Laney a complete and unconditional pardon, with the stipulation that he'd become a railroad detective."

Flagle nodded agreement. "All you'd have had to do was be at the meeting and take him into custody. Everything was prearranged."

"I'm aware of all the finagling," Titus said. "The arrangement was a treacherous one, a setup offering him amnesty with the firm intention of making him prisoner when he showed up for the parley. I'd have nothing to do with that, as a matter of principle."

"Laney was warned off. I've often wondered who tipped our hand."

Titus was silent, busy with a sudden flood of memories.

He had no guilt feelings about his last face-to-face meeting with Laney. At that time he'd told Bart of the plot to capture and imprison him through the underhanded way of offering him a complete pardon for his past sins, plus future employment with the railroad. He remembered the meeting with Bart vividly, as though it had happened yesterday. He recalled it now with a sense of failure on both sides of his nature, that of lawman opposed to brotherly feelings.

Their last agreement, a truce as it were, took place at night at a lonely railroad siding, near a water tank. He remembered the bright moon, the water dripping from the wooden tank sounding unnaturally loud. Bart rode out of the night and dismounted. Titus, waiting, holding his horse, spoke first. "Howdy, Bart."

"Howdy, Will."

They were silent for a long period, looking at one another, each concealing his innermost thoughts. Finally it was Titus who broke the silence. "How's it feel to be leaving a life of crime?"

Bart laughed. He always laughed, at everything and everybody. "It'll be some different. The big boys made an offer I couldn't turn down."

"An unconditional pardon and gainful legal employment with the railroad?"

"You got it right, Will. That's about the size of it. The railroad president has made me personal guarantees."

"You've thought this out carefully, I take it?"

"Yep. Robbin' banks and railroads is gettin' riskier all the time. If I keep on it's just a matter of time until I get killed or go to jail, either of which I'm plumb dead against." He leaned forward. "What's this all about, Will?"

"I wanted you to know it's all a trap," Titus said. "You give yourself up and you'll go to jail, Bart, or get yourself killed."

For once Bart didn't laugh. Titus thought he detected a slight lowering of his shoulders. After a long silence, he said, "Is that a fact, Will?"

"That's a fact," Titus said firmly.

"Why'd you take the trouble to keep me out o' trouble?"

"I owe you one. That time, up at Coyote Creek, behind the beaver dam. Where we used to swim in the summer."

"I remember. That big red horse of yours liked to swim as much as we did. Until he got tangled up in them lily pads. Went loco, he did, and you got hit from a hock or a hoof. Lyin' there, face down in the water, Will, I thought you was a goner. Towed you in to the shore by the hair of your head. It all comes back to me like yesterday."

"That's one reason I'm telling you about this trap," Titus said evenly. "You saved my life."

"You got more than one reason?"

"Yes. I'll have no part in a treacherous scheme such as they've got planned for taking you into custody."

"Well, that's mighty square of you. I'm sorry in a way, and I'm glad in a way. I kind of like the outlaw life. Free and easy, lots of boodle and plenty of good times. Seems now I don't have to decide for myself. It's good to have them things decided for me, ain't it, Will?"

Titus was silent, thinking that what he had wanted to do was hug Bart, hug him and tell him he loved him. That time was too far in the distant past and he couldn't form the words through the emotion swelling his chest and making an ache in his throat.

Bart gathered his reins. "Thanks, Will," he said, low-voiced, mounted and turned his horse.

Titus forced himself to say, "Good luck, Bart. Keep an eye out."

Flagle brought Titus back to the present. "Have a cigar, Titus," he said, holding out a silver case.

Titus looked at the cigars, brown and fat, a good brand he recognized. He hesitated for a moment and then shook his head. "Thanks, no. Thanks anyway."

Flagle extracted a cigar from the case. After replacing the case in an inside coat pocket he bit off the end of the cigar and spat it out. He found a match, struck it and lighted up.

Titus drew the drifting smoke deep into his lungs, savoring the heady aroma.

"I'll try to be honest, Titus," Flagle said when the cigar was drawing to his satisfaction. "I'm sort of pulled this way and that about you. On the one hand I wish you were like most of my other marshals, tending to paperwork and such, and leaving the law enforcement duties to their deputies. Why didn't you delegate this job to your deputies? You've plenty of competent men under your supervision, Titus."

Titus nodded. "There's a reason, of course. Bart Laney is not your run-of-the-mill outlaw. He's a folk hero of sorts in this area. He's looked upon as a kind of Robin Hood. Even the sheriffs like him. Most of the law enforcement officers wouldn't cross the street to take Laney into custody. That goes for my deputies. Therefore, I felt it necessary to take on the job myself."

"But he robs banks and railroads and company payrolls."

"The average citizen doesn't give a hoot for that. The banks and railroads are so gouging and oppressive, our people out here in the west secretly enjoy it when Laney makes a good haul."

"I was somewhat aware of that," Flagle nodded, looking at the tip of his cigar. "I'm glad to hear you say it."

"You'll use it against me?"

Flagle nodded regretfully. "If you don't saddle up and head for Tucson prior to my departure, I'll begin proceedings to remove you from office on my return to Washington. I hate to do it but there's no other way for me."

"If Laney shows up I'll take him," Titus said.

"A personal vendetta?"

"I believe not."

"Has it anything to do with the Circle Valley Massacre?"

A sudden wind whipped up, swirling dust in the street, moving the poplar trees and whisking away Flagle's cigar ashes. He gave Titus a keen look. "You were probably not born when that happened. What's your interest, if any?"

"I was alive all right. I was one of the seven survivors of the massacre, Chief Flagle. Less than a year old. Matthew Laney took me in and raised me with Bart. We were of the same age." And Martha nursed you, he told himself, at the same time she nursed Bart.

"I should think you'd be grateful for being nurtured by the Laney family."

"It's a long story, a very long one, and not a story I'm inclined to discuss."

Flagle made motions of departure: rising, dusting cigar ashes from his coat. He settled his hat more firmly on his head against the rising wind and stood up in the dirt looking up at Titus. "My advice to you is go back to Tucson."

"You have my answer. I'm curious to know where you're staying while you're here? In what home?"

Flagle shrugged. "Bishop Cantrell offered me food and shelter. In all good conscience I had to refuse his hospitality. I'm riding to Richfield immediately, where I'll turn in this sorry horse I'm riding to the livery stable. I'll get on the train there and be back in Washington within a week." He finished speaking and stiffened as Pierpont came from the fruit orchard with a string of fish. "What have we here?"

"He's a photographer," Titus said. "Makes pictures, so he says. The Laneys gave him permission to camp in the orchard."

"Keep an eye on him," warned Flagle.

Pierpont crossed the irrigation ditch and then the road, angling toward them. He was in a state of mild excitement. "Say, look, I caught these trout in an irrigation ditch back up there. Nice, aren't they?"

Titus and Flagle looked at the man in silence.

"What I meant to ask was, I've more than I need. Would you care for some?"

"I'm leaving," Flagle said.

"No, thank you," Titus responded.

"Well, I must say that's too bad. After I cook them up perhaps I may offer a few to your prisoners?"

"Stay away from my prisoners."

"Ah, if you say so, sir."

"I say so," Titus said firmly.

The photographer, somewhat embarrassed, turned away. "Well, thought I'd ask," he muttered, and retreated toward the orchard.

"Better watch that one," Flagle said and did not offer his hand before striding to his horse. He mounted with some difficulty due to his bulk, reined the horse around and headed north without looking back.

Titus watched him out of sight, speculating that the President of the United States must have a lot of spare time on his hands personally to dispatch his Chief Marshal to conduct such a parley as the one just ended.

The sky darkened and gray-black clouds boiled overhead while thunder rumbled threateningly. A bolt of lightning split the sky and hit a nearby tree, splintering it with an ear-splitting crash. The horses in the corral behind Grafton's house neighed in terror as hail the size of hens' eggs fell out of the sky, bouncing on the road, raising dust while the prisoners roared in pain.

Titus walked to the end of the porch and watched his horse, Peso, and Grafton's buggy horse circling the corral in tail-raised terror, the whites of their eyes showing their fright.

He adjusted his hat, preparatory to making a dash to the corral when the front door opened and Jenny Gardner emerged in a rush. Plainly, she was frightened. She looked soundlessly at his empty rocking chair, then her gaze shifted to him and she ran to him, clutching at him with her hands, huddling close to him as though for protection. "I—I'm scared to death of storms," she said, flinching as another roll of thunder sounded and vivid lightning put their shadows on the wall for a brief moment.

He had his arms around her, holding her to him and finding her soft curves stirring him almost as much as her helplessness. "Nothing to worry about," he said.

"Can't help myself." Her teeth chattered. "Been that way since a little girl."

He led her to the rocking chair. "I got to get those damn fool horses under shelter," he said. "They'll break out if I don't."

"I'll go with you!"

"No, these hailstones will put knots on your head. Maybe knock you unconscious."

"I'll hold your saddlebags over me," she said and attempted to lift the bags from the floor.

"They're filled with ammunition," he said. "Stay put and you'll be all right."

He hit the ground running and didn't take the time to open the gate but vaulted the fence. He got a hand on the hacka-mores of both horses and led them back under the corner shelter and secured them. He stood then for a moment, watching the hailstones accumulate into an icy mass. He ran back to the porch and Jenny again ran to him. He held her while staring across the road. The prisoners had removed the skin screen from their sanitary pit and squatted on their hunkers, holding the screen over their heads for protection.

As quickly as it started the storm clouds moved over and passed. The hail gradually diminished and finally ceased, to be replaced by a downpour of fat raindrops that lasted only a few minutes.

Jenny moved tentatively away from Titus, not looking at him but keeping her head down. "I'm sorry," she said. "I just couldn't help myself." She moved another step away. "I better get on with my housework." She turned and disappeared through the door but Titus kept remembering the feel of her body pressed against his. He caught a flash of movement from the Laney house and saw Elizabeth's face for a moment before the curtain dropped.

The cloud mass moved rapidly north, the thunder muted now, and with only an occasional flash of distant lightning. To the south shafts of sunlight appeared, emerging from breaks in the clouds and laying golden columns of sunlight on the wet earth.

He motioned to the prisoners to replace the screen and when they had done so he returned to his chair and resumed his watch.

Come on, Bart, come on down, he thought with savage intensity.

Jenny emerged from the house and stopped beside his chair. She leaned over and placed a bowl on his knee. "Some chicken and dumplings," she said. "It's not fit to eat. I was cooking them when that awful storm hit and the fire went out. But I done the best I could."

"As always," Titus answered. "It'll be just about perfect."

"And tell Brother Grafton his supper's in the warmer."

"He never comes in by the front door anymore."

"Oh, that poor man, my heart bleeds for him. This town will never be the same."

"It couldn't get any worse," Titus said, "so whatever happens it'll be an improvement."

"I declare, Will Titus. You say something nice and then spoil it a minute later."

"Voicing my considered opinion," he said, tasting the dumpling. "Just as I said, it's delicious."

"Well, eat it all." She gave the ties to her sunbonnet a tug and went down the steps and headed south. He watched her go with a feeling of loneliness that wasn't new to him.

CHAPTER 15

Bart Laney sat on a log near the campfire which smouldered in front of the log cabin at the outlaw hideout. A haunch of venison was spitted over the hot ashes and now and then Willie gave it a turn to keep it from burning. The odor of cooking deer meat pervaded the air. Ellie Bay lounged on the other side of the fire, tossing twigs into the hot ashes. A stud game was going on near the cabin, four men sitting cross-legged on a blanket. The atmosphere was one of relaxation.

"It's a rough show, Bart," Ellie Bay said. "We'll do whatever you want done but we got to know what it is you want."

The short, plump man turning the haunch of venison nodded. "Yeah, Bart, you know we'll do whatever we hafta, just say the word."

"Goddamn it, Willie," Ellie said, "quit messin' with that hunk of meat. Go do something, move the horses to better grass, any damn thing."

"All right, Ellie," Willie said in a mild voice and moved over to the poker game and stood looking down at the play.

"You're tough on him," Laney said.

"Maybe." Ellie Bay threw a quick look at Willie, who had rushed to tattle to Bart about Gorila. "You're not holdin' it against me for sendin' Gorila down?"

Laney denied it with a shake of his head. "No, Ellie. Forget it."

"I'm wonderin' what's botherin' you."

"I'm kind of wonderin' myself," Laney answered with a crooked grin. A compact man, muscular and active, he dominated without giving offense. He had no worries about the loyalties of the men who followed him. Many outlaws throughout the west yearned to join Laney's gang but it was not easy to do. "Ellie, I can read your mind. You want to go down there and kill Will Titus and get it over with. When that happens the U. S. Government will send in every damn marshal west of the Mississippi into this country."

"I thought you didn't want him killed for personal reasons."

"There's that, too. Let's wait for Brace. When he gets here we can find out what's best for all."

Laney was thinking back to the time that Will's uncle, Seth Titus, had come from Arkansas to get custody of Will. It was near the same time that Matthew Laney had been executed for his part in the Circle Valley Massacre. It had been a hard and sorrow-filled time for the Laney family, particularly difficult for Bart in losing a beloved brother, namely Will Titus. That bitter period was a dominant factor in his life, when a transient bucking horse show came to Circle City. The fast-talking showman had a bucking horse he claimed no man had ever rode. He offered a prize of a silver-mounted saddle to anyone riding the animal, a tall, strong sorrel with wild eyes and an unremitting hatred of man that vented itself in a fury of explosive muscle-powered action when a rider touched its back.

Bart paid his five dollar entry fee and rode the tall sorrel to a standstill before a small crowd across the river from Grafton's mill on the Troublesome River. The man with the string of bucking horses refused to give Bart the saddle and the youngster took it from him at gunpoint. When the showman complained, the sheriff at Richfield rode over to ask Bart a few questions. Bart lit out for the Cedar Breaks before the sheriff arrived. The damn saddle turned green before he got well into outlaw country.

That started him on the owl hoot, where he gained as much notoriety as Jesse James. He closed his eyes, remembering the youthful cattle rustling, graduation to bigger jobs. He remembered the trains he'd robbed, the banks he'd held up, the company payrolls he'd heisted, all of them generating more public attention, but without killing a fellow human being.

"Here comes Brace now," Ellie Bay said, rising and staring down the trail.

Brace Bowman rode his horse straight to the campfire and dismounted, removing his hat and beating the dust from his clothing. Willie came over and took the reins from him and led Bowman's thoroughbred toward the rope corral.

Brace put his hat back on and took out a pocket knife and opened a long blade. He leaned over and carved a slice of meat from the haunch of venison. He closed the knife and squatted before the fire, eating the meat stolidly, his eyes on the ashes of the fire. "Not too bad," he said. "Willie must a killed that deer and took care of it."

Bay nodded. "Yeah, he goes through a big rigamarole when he shoots a deer."

"You can tell it in the eatin', too," Brace said, poking the last shred of meat in his mouth and wiping his hands on a handkerchief from his hip pocket. He looked at Bart. "You heard all that stuff about Buffalo Bill and Mark Twain comin' to see Titus?"

"I heard."

"Well, the latest is the Chief U.S. Marshal, a big pot-gutted man named Flagle. He come to Circle City all the way from Washington, D.C., to send Titus back to Arizona."

"And Titus refused to go?"

"Aw, shoot, how'd you know?"

"I know Will pretty good. What's going on down there besides that?"

"This Flagle, the top hand of the marshals, he said he was gonna fire Titus when he got back to Washington, D.C. Titus acted like his business would all be finished by the time Flagle could officially fire him."

Laney was silent, looking at Brace, waiting for him to continue. The poker game broke up and the players drifted over to the fire and stood silently watching.

"The bishopric's got all kind a plans, Bart," Brace went on, "none of them nailed down right now. Cantrell's got some Danites comin' in not only to remove Titus from the land o' the livin', but to clean out Gentility, our very own Sodom and Gomorrah."

"I had hoped they'd have a better plan than the Danites."

Brace nodded. "They have, all right. Bishop Cantrell wants you to come on down and see which one you like. They want you to show just after dark tonight, and go to the sheep wagon alongside the new church they're buildin'. You start now you'll make it before moon-up."

Laney rose and stretched. He looked around at the group of men watching him in silent anticipation. "You, Lefty, and you, Sam, come with me. The rest of you stay close to camp 'til I get word to you."

"I'll saddle your hoss," Willie said and went toward the rope corral.

"Get me a fresh one," Brace called. "I'll be leadin' the horse I rode in on."

"Sho' nuff," Willie called cheerfully.

Ellie Bay and the men left with him watched as Laney and his three companions rode down the trail. When they disappeared in a fold of the mountain, he said, "That might be the last time we'll see him. He's gonna get killed or taken by Titus sure as wolves howl."

The men looked at him owlishly. "One's same as t'other."

"That's what I'm talkin' about. Now, question is, what do we do if we lose Bart?"

"I hate to even think about it."

Bay nodded. "We got to think about it. I'm gettin' sick and tired of doodlin' around up here on the mountain, waitin' for somethin' to happen. Sick and tired, that's what."

"Spit it out, Ellie, what's on your mind?"

"We better just write Bart off. First off, let's go down there and get Gorila loose. We might have to kill Titus doin' it, but what the hell is one marshal more or less."

"Listen, Ellie, what'll Bart—"

Bay said savagely, "Don't give me no trouble, Willie. Like I said, we might as well write Bart off."

"I'm not writin' Bart off," Willie muttered.

"Then you stand by yourself," Bay said. He looked around the circle of faces. "Right, boys?"

After a moment of hesitation they all nodded uncertainly.

"We'll move out right away and get closer t' town," Bay said. "We can camp in one a them shallow draws north of the graveyard an' see what we can do to get Gorila loose."

"What 'bout them other two chained up with Gorila?"

"They can come in if they want to," Bay said. "We got plenty extra guns. Let's go."

"Bart'd never let the likes o' Shagrun and Kile in his bunch," Willie said.

"Shut your goddamned yap," Bay said.

Willie sat by the fire silently watching them as they saddled their horses. He didn't move to wave a farewell when the horsemen filed down the mountainside.

Down below, Bay pulled in his horse. "You fellers just walk your horses on," he said. "I gotta tell Willie somethin'." He turned his horse and rode back into camp. Willie still sat beside the fire. He rose as Bay brought his horse close to the fire and stopped, looking stonily down at him.

"I know what's on your mind, Ellie," Willie said in a toneless voice, taking a step backward. "Get on with it if that's what you come back for."

"I'm gonna take over from Bart," Bay said, "no matter what happens. I'm afraid you'd always be in the way, little feller."

"I sure think a heap o' Bart," Willie said. "I'll stick by him long as I live. Just like he'd stick by me."

"Well, damn it, I can't help you, then," Bay said and pulled his pistol and fired point-blank into Willie's chest. Red blossomed on Willie's shirt front as he backpedaled, his arms waving wildly as though to balance himself, until he fell on his back, sighing, and then a groan that subsided abruptly, as he lay still, his pistol untouched in its holster.

Blowing into the muzzle of his pistol, Bay urged his mount forward with his knees and looked down at Willie. "Pore damn fool," he muttered as he ejected a spent shell. Reloading his Colt, he turned his horse and without a backward glance rode down the mountain.

CHAPTER 16

A rooster crowing in the early predawn brought Titus out of his bedroll. He pulled on his boots, clapped his hat on his head, rolled up his soogan and placed it on the porch. Making a swift circuit by the smithy where the prisoners still slept, he found all quiet; and he tramped to the creek for his morning ablution.

Returning to the house, he stopped by the corral as Peso thrust his head over the top rail. The gelding had rolled in the dirt and detritus of the storm had matted his hide with a rough coating. He put a lead rope on the horse and led it to the porch and tied up. Getting a curry comb and brush from his belongings, he began working while Peso whickered softly, jerking his head toward the corral where Grafton's buggy horse was exhibiting signs of resentment at the separation.

Working on Peso, all the while keeping a vigilant lookout, he gradually restored a shine to the usually sleek hide. He was finishing off with the brush when a movement on the first rise of land beyond the Laney house caused him to freeze. He stepped up on the porch with the brush in his hand for a better look. The sun edged over the rim of distant mountains, flooding the rough desolate country with a revealing light. A man on a horse stopped, skylining himself for a considerable time before dismounting.

Titus exchanged the brush for a telescope, adjusted it and resting it against a porch support, picked up the distant rider, standing beside his horse. Big, bearded and burly the man appeared to be in no hurry, standing there, gazing toward Titus. As Titus watched the stranger turned to his horse and Titus stiffened, expecting the unknown rider to draw the saddle gun from its scabbard. It was not a rifle but a long glass the man turned on Titus. They stared at one another through their telescopes, each studying the other. The distance was too great for accurate carbine shooting which was the reason Titus had not grabbed his rifle instead of the telescope. The long-barreled Sharps he'd taken from the Fenton kid would easily make the distance but Titus had not seen a Sharps in the stranger's gear. The stranger's mount moved and Titus saw a packhorse that had been hidden behind the unusually large riding horse. He could see the high jutting stock of a Sharps projecting above the pack. A Sharps was a hard gun to conceal. Apparently the man had no intention of using the long rifle for he put his glass away and began unsaddling his horse. He put the animal on a rope and picket pin and then went to the pack animal and unlashed the load and let it drop to the ground. He made no move to make camp but centered his attention on Titus. Titus stepped to the ground, finished grooming Peso and turned the animal back into the corral.

Returning to the porch, he continued to watch the stranger who stood motionless looking down into the valley. Titus' uneasiness deepened.

Jason approached on the road in his usual stiff-legged walk when passing Titus. "Come here, boy."

Startled, Jason turned abruptly, tripping over his own feet. "Yes, sir," he said, and trotted obediently into the yard, his eyes anxiously searching Titus' face.

"See that fellow up there on the ridge?" Titus asked, pointing.

Jason turned and looked and looked at Titus over his shoulder, "Yes, sir. I see him all right."

"Fine. Jump on Peso and ride up there and tell that man to come down here and make his intentions known."

"Me? Me ride your horse?"

"Yes, you. Now get moving."

"What if he don't want to come down?"

"Tell him I'll shoot his riding horse if he doesn't get moving toward me at the count of ten after you get there. And then I'll shoot his pack animal. Now hustle."

"I'll saddle up."

"Don't take the time. Ride Peso bareback and hurry now." Titus picked up the Sharps and checked it to make certain it was loaded. He got another piece of brass from his saddlebags and slipped it in his coat pocket.

Jason led a reluctant Peso into the yard while Grafton's buggy mare ran back and forth in the corral whinnying. Jason jumped up and threw a leg over Peso's back and the horse gave a few short hops and Jason fell off. Peso stood quietly as Jason got up, dusting his pants off.

"Just feeling his oats," Titus said. "Get back on him and let him know who's boss."

"Yes, sir," Jason said shakily and again mounted Peso and clapped his legs against Peso's sides and squeaked, "Durn you, giddap!"

"Get up, Peso," Titus said in a firm voice. "Get outta here, boy!"

Peso bolted away with Jason holding the reins in one hand, the other hand wrapped in Peso's mane.

"Ride him hard, Jason," Titus called. "He needs the exercise." He watched as Peso pounded down the road with Jason pulling on the reins, making a circle around Laney's fruit orchard. The photographer ran out to watch.

Jason disappeared from Titus' sight for a few minutes and then reappeared as he emerged on higher ground. Peso went smoothly up the rise in a hard run. Jason had lost his hat and his hair flew wildly, stirred by the wind and Peso's run. The photographer turned back into the grove of trees.

The big man on the ridge came slowly to meet Jason. He stood steady as the horse flung itself to a sliding halt, with Jason slipping up on its neck. Continuing to watch, Titus saw Jason gesturing toward the valley, leaning forward. The big man looked long and intently at Titus and then went to his horse and bridled and saddled it. Mounting, he followed Jason who headed back the way he'd come.

Jason trotted Peso into Grafton's yard, followed by the big man on a large, strong horse. "There's the man," Jason said, "Mr. Frederic Remington."

"How do," Titus said, lifting his shotgun as the big man dismounted and nodded to Titus.

"He ain't no gunslinger," Jason said. "He's an artist, the most famous artist in the world."

"Did he tell you that?"

"Heck, no, I knew who he was when he said what his name is."

The big bearded man said, "Hell, fire, Marshal, don't you trust nobody?"

"Very few."

"Maybe I know what you mean. I'm getting an education I didn't get in college. I've just been done out of my place up in Kansas by a couple of scalawags and it nearly ruined my trust in human nature."

"I have to be careful," Titus said, shifting the Greener to a better position. "Are you armed?"

"I thought everybody went armed in this territory," Remington said. He came forward and stood at the edge of the porch. "Mind if I sit?"

Titus nodded and Remington sat on the edge of the porch as Jason edged forward, his face alight with admiration and awe. "If you're nervous, Marshal, I'll hang my weapon on my saddle horn 'til I'm ready to leave."

"Never mind. I warn you that trouble may break out any minute. If that happens I'll not be responsible for your well-being."

"I accept that," Remington said easily. "What I want to do is sketch you, Marshal Titus. And do a full scale painting later on. That's how I usually work."

"Why would you want to sketch me?"

"You're a famous man, Marshal. You're in all the newspapers

and magazines. The nation follows your adventures and can't get enough of it. *Harper's Weekly* wants me to sketch you for their magazine."

"They pay you for that?" Titus asked. To Jason he said, "Rub Peso down, Jason, and turn him back in the corral."

"Yes, sir," Jason said reluctantly, and walked toward the corral, leading the horse.

"They pay me," Remington said shortly. "Same as you get paid for capturing dangerous criminals."

"There's a slight difference." He studied the artist for a moment and then added: "What you did was cause me some concern about your intentions, Mr. Remington, not knowing you from Adam's off ox. I can't have people setting up a shooting gallery to pick me off. I did see a Sharps in your pack."

"I have a Sharps rifle," Remington admitted. "I thought maybe I'd bag a buffalo on the way out here. Didn't see a single beast."

"They're getting scarce." Titus stood up. "Now that I know what you're about you may resume your activity."

"You'll let me sketch you?"

"You can do as you please, but do it from a distance. I can tolerate no distractions."

Remington nodded and rising, strode to his horse. He mounted, touched his hat brim and rode out of the yard. Pierpont came out of the orchard and hailed Remington and the big man turned his horse in that direction.

Titus ignored them as Jason came around the corner of the house and stopped short. "Shoot, he's gone!"

"No, he's over there talking to Pierpont," Titus said, pointing.

"Hot dog, maybe I'll get to talk to him."

"Sounds like he might be a talker," Titus said dryly. "You better get on to Grafton's. Tell him I sent you on an errand if he complains of your being late."

"Thanks, Marshal," Jason said as he trotted away.

"I appreciate you giving old Peso a workout," Titus called and Jason waved and trotted on.

Pierpont and Remington disappeared into the orchard. Later, Titus observed Remington moving his pack horse into the fruit orchard. He felt a twinge of loneliness somewhere inside himself.

A young boy came to feed the prisoners. A hack, pulled by a pair of sleek bay horses, moved slowly past. The hack was loaded with six ladies of the night from Gentility, dressed in all their finery and holding parasols. A shout went up from the prisoners and calls went back and forth. The hack proceeded up the road and circled in front of Grafton's store and returned. The hack made two passes, creating a greater disturbance among the prisoners with each trip.

Sighing, Titus walked to the edge of the road and held up his hand. The hack driver, a derby-hatted man with a cigar in his mouth, said, "Yeah, Marshal?"

"You're creating a disturbance," Titus said. "It'd be a big favor to me if you'd get the hell out of town." He stared, holding the driver's glance.

"Digger, let's go," one of the girls said in a pleading voice.

Another, even more frightened, shrilled: "Go on, Digger, do what she says!"

"What, get run outta town by a two-bit marshal?"

Digger, apparently a gambler by trade as evidenced by his white, well-cared-for hands holding the lines, considered himself a tough nut, equal to any challenge. He leaned sideways, his cigar at a pugnacious angle, preparing for Titus' response. What Digger saw was a cold-eyed man with no trace of excitement on his forbidding face, only a clear readiness for violence. Digger felt his insides suddenly crumble; he fought a losing battle against being humbled before the dance hall girls. He made his decision, straightened, threw away his cigar and lifted the lines. "Guess you're right, Abigail," he said and clucked to his team and moved on.

The blonde lady who had first warned Digger gave Titus an enticing glance over her shoulder. "You get through here, Marshal, come on over to Gentility. Ask for Trixie."

"Shut up, damn you!" Digger muttered.

Pierpont ran out of the orchard with a tripod over his shoulder, shouting, "Wait up there, wait a minute, please!"

Remington followed, more slowly, carrying a bulky bag which Titus assumed held photographic equipment. He felt a tinge of discontent that the two men had struck it off so well and so soon.

Digger stopped the team, waiting. Pierpont panted up, saying, "Sorry to delay you but I wanted to take a picture of you and the ladies talking to the Marshal."

"To hell with that," Digger said and slapped his reins against the horses' rumps and moved them into a trot. Over his shoulder he called, "You wanna take pictures come to the Square Deal in Gentility. We can talk turkey there."

Pierpont stood staring after the departing hack. He turned and walked down the middle of the road, turning in toward Titus as Remington joined him.

"Marshal, why'd that man leave in such a hurry?" Pierpont asked.

"He might have been creating a diversion," Titus said. "I can't allow any such thing to happen."

"I wanted to take a picture of those soiled doves," Pierpont complained. He turned to Remington. "Maybe you could sketch 'em from memory, Frederick?"

Remington shook his shaggy head. "I simply can't sketch a female," he admitted. "I tried to once and had to wash her out before the painting was finished."

"Damnation!" Pierpont muttered.

"You two take your gear and sashay back into that orchard," Titus ordered. "I'm becoming a little weary of all this commotion."

Remington began framing a protest but Pierpont lifted his tripod to his shoulder and hastily departed. After a short period of silence, Remington asked quietly, "What's eating on you, Marshal?"

"That is none of your damn business."

Remington shrugged his massive shoulders and turned away to follow Pierpont back among the trees.

Later, Jenny Gardner came, carrying a bunch of greens in her apron, the dew still glistening on the rough leaves. She paused on the steps, looking at Titus with that school-teacherish look she adopted at times. "You're abusing the Lord's patience," she said.

"Who said that?"

"Bishop Cantrell himself."

"He left part of it out," Titus responded. "Did you see the crowd from Gentility?"

"Yes, I did, much as I tried not to look."

"Don't close your eyes to what goes on in the world," Titus advised. "It's not the looking or not looking that changes things."

"Oh, pshaw. Speaking of looking, if you'll look in the hen-house for fresh eggs I'll fry a couple for your breakfast."

"I've had breakfast, thank you."

"That awful jerky? You'll starve on food like that."

"It's carried me a long way. Don't worry."

"You can't leave that rocker long enough to gather a few eggs for your very own good."

"You may be right, Mrs. Gardner," he said formally.

Her face tightened and she entered the house slamming the door with unnecessary force.

Titus had made patience his ally but that was wearing thin. Surveying the distant mountains which probably sheltered Bart at this very moment, he could see no movement at all other than the flight of an eagle out in the vast distances that seemed to diminish him as a man. He'd almost forgotten the raw and savage beauty of this land but it came back to him all of a sudden. His memory played tricks on him by turning his thoughts inward to forbidden territory, all of this brought on by this strange land which was yet so familiar to him.

CHAPTER 17

Bart Laney and Brace Bowman rode ahead of Lefty and Sam, Bart hardly aware of his riding companions. His thoughts darted here and there, back to the past, involving Titus, flitting to the present, also picturing Titus. The brush and trees thinned out as they neared the point where the canyon emptied onto the benchland. Bart could see lights of Circle City in the far distance, a yellow twinkle here and there, lights that gradually winked out, one by one, as he rode. With the last light out the valley was a dark void, limned by the mountains, and the heavens alight with stars. He remembered the time he and Will Titus camped in a grassy mountain meadow. After supper, their blankets on the ground, they lay on their backs, looked up through the fir branches at the sky, speculating on the meaning of all that was before them. "What the hell," he muttered.

"You say somethin'?" Brace asked.

"Nothing. Nothing important."

"You should a brought Ellie with you."

"He's all right, Brace. I'm not worried about Ellie."

"He's gettin' awful restless. Can't make no money sittin' on a mountain."

"Willie tell you that?"

"Yeah, well, sure. But he didn't have to tell me."

The riders crossed an irrigation ditch between the upper and lower reservoirs. Bart heard fish flopping around in the flooded field below him and smelled the odor of water on dry earth. He had seen nothing since leaving the hideout but his caution had not slackened. The wind shifted to the southwest and came in a fresher gust, and then blew steadily. He reined in suddenly when he heard a woman's voice.

"Bart, wait. It's me."

Elizabeth. He looked to his right from which direction the voice had come. They all waited, leather creaking, bridle chains tinkling as she rode out of the night to stop beside Bart. She leaned toward him for his quick kiss and a touch of his hand. Lefty and Sam uncocked their weapons and the sound seemed unusually loud in the night.

"How's Ma?"

"Same, Bart. No change. She's waiting."

He kept silent for a long moment, then hesitantly asked, "What about Will?"

"He's there," she said simply.

"He'll be there when the cows come home," Brace said.

"Let's go." Bart put his horse in motion. Elizabeth rode beside him. Brace drifted back to ride with Lefty and Sam.

"Who's down there?" Bart asked after a time of silence.

"Cantrell, Grafton. Yes, and Lucian."

"We don't want to keep the good bishop waiting."

"He is an impatient man."

"What's on his mind?"

"I don't know all of it. But there's a bunch of Danites camped on the north side of town."

"I don't like it."

"You won't like this either," Elizabeth said. "Cantrell's moving the women and children out tomorrow."

"What's he plannin' to do, burn the town?"

"No, there's no telling what he means to do but it all adds up to big trouble. I've heard that when the Danites finish Will, they're going on to Gentility to burn that place to the ground."

"Don't they ever learn anything?"

They circled the town and came in from the north, stopping beside the sheep wagon which was dark. Dave Grubbs, the stonemason, had heard them coming and was lighting a lantern. He opened the door of the sheep wagon and placed the lighted lantern on the floor, backed off and looked at Elizabeth. "You don't need me," he said. "I'll bunk in Cantrell's barn tonight."

"Good night, Dave," she said as he disappeared in the night. She dismounted.

Bart put his hand on his saddle horn and stepped to the ground, passing his reins to Lefty. "Put 'em all in Cantrell's barn," he said, "but don't unsaddle. Just loosen the cinches and give 'em a bait of grain."

"Not mine," Brace said. "I'm gonna stay at my ma's tonight."

"Might as well go on over, Brace," Bart said. "I'll see you come morning."

Brace rode off into the night, leading his favorite riding horse. Lefty and Sam went toward Cantrell's leading the horses.

Bart opened the door of the sheep wagon when three men came out of the night, silent and morose.

"Get the lantern, Bart," Cantrell said, "and come on over here." He walked on past the sheep wagon to where a flatbed wagon stood, the one used to haul stone from the quarry site to the building. Taking the lantern from Bart, Cantrell squatted and thrust the light forward, revealing the possum belly. "We got this rigged strong enough to hold you," he said. "You crawl in there tomorrow early, and we'll drive the rig into Lucian's, pretending repairs are needed. After dark you get out and crawl in the coffin. Next morning we'll carry the coffin into the house. With you in it."

Bart squatted silently for a long running moment while Elizabeth and the men stared at him. Lefty and Sam came into the circle and silently joined the watchers.

Standing, Bart hitched his belt and said, "Is that the best you can do?"

"We've thought of everything," Cantrell said. "We've run out of ideas, Bart."

"What about the Danites?"

"They're here. And they're ready."

"Ready for what?"

"To do what has to be done, smite the Lord's enemies." Cantrell spoke in his most sonorous tone.

Bart shook his head. "I'm not fixing to sneak around to do what I have to do."

"There's something—" Elizabeth began but Cantrell cut her off with a brusque: "Keep your silence, woman."

"Let her have her say." Bart's tone forbade argument.

"It's about Will," Elizabeth said hurriedly. "He's crippled in his right hand, Bart. I don't know why but he can't shoot or do much of anything with his right hand."

"How'd you find out about that?"

"I was there when someone shot at him. A bushwhacker out in our fruit orchard. Will drew his gun from a shoulder holster with his left hand and returned the fire."

"Did he get the ambusher?"

"No, but I learned he shoots now with his left hand. I've noticed him massaging his right wrist from time to time. Maybe Doctor Mac would know."

"If he did he wouldn't tell," Bart said. He stood there his head drooped, silent, moody.

"You'll not have a need to face Titus, Bart," Cantrell said impatiently. "Let the Danites deal with him."

"Yes, let the Danites do it," Grafton urged.

"I'd rather they didn't."

"They came here to fight. They expect to fight. They're ready. I may not be able to deter them."

"Bart, why don't you follow the bishop's plan and go in like he said. It'll work," Elizabeth said.

"No, I'm not about to do it that way."

"Then what are you going to do?" Cantrell asked in a vexed tone.

Bart said, "I been killing my own snakes too long to let somebody else do it. The Danites worry me. They get started no telling what might happen. You try to stop them, Bishop

Cantrell. What I'm going to do, I'll do it without any help and in my own sweet time."

Elizabeth felt her eyes sting with unshed tears and her throat tightened. "I've got to get back to Mama," she said and turned away.

"Tell her I'll see her first thing in the morning," Bart called and went off into the darkness in the opposite direction from that Elizabeth had taken.

Elizabeth walked through the night toward her home and now the tears came freely. She cried quietly and without trying to restrain herself. After all this time of worry and frustration she felt the need for release. She took it in the only way she knew how, with tears. I'm foolish, she thought, to believe I could change anything.

She slowed her steps as she approached the darkened blacksmith shop, the ridge of the old barn looming above the outlined mountains in the far distance. She could hear Pierpont and Remington laughing and talking in their camp in the orchard. Their campfire cast a faint glow on the trees. The prisoners were quiet and she assumed they were asleep. She stopped suddenly when she heard a soft stifled cough in the darkness. She froze, her eyes searching the night, her ears suddenly tuned to catch any sound. She waited, stilling her breathing to a mere whisper. She decided that the sound was that of a coyote that had wandered into town searching for food, or one of the many pigs roaming the town since Riley was killed. A form rose out of the darkness and she smelled the rankness of the man as he seized her and placed a hard hand over her mouth before she could scream.

"Don't make a peep," a hoarse voice whispered, "an' I won't hurt you." He forced her ahead of him, keeping his hand over her mouth in a tight grip. He twisted her around and passed from the road before reaching Grafton's darkened store. There was a pile of rubbish behind the store and a brushy tree Grafton had brought down from the mountains and planted there to hide the rubble. Two men were there and it was Ellie Bay who came to meet them.

"What the hell is this?" Ellie Bay asked in a hoarse whisper.

"She run into me down by the blacksmith shop."

Bay struck a match and held it up briefly. He swore: "Dammit, this is Bart's sister—"

"Oh, shoot, I didn't know—" Elizabeth's captor removed his hand from her mouth. "I'm purely sorry, ma'am. I didn't—"

"You already said you didn't know," Ellie Bay said angrily. "Why in hell can't you do a simple little thing like getting the lay of the land?"

"I done talked to them bozos chained up like you told me to, Ellie, an' I didn't tip off Titus, either. Them three are not so anxious to get away. They gettin' three squares a day and they figger when Titus is killed or takes Bart they'll be let go. I started tellin' 'em about making a haul up Rock Springs way, and then them big nights in Fort Worth, and they decided they do wanna be let go."

"I'll be leaving now," Elizabeth said. "My mother is home alone. She's helpless."

"Shut up," Bay said. "Lemme think."

"Don't tell me to shut up," Elizabeth said, "just let me alone."

"So you can run to Titus?"

"Will's mad at me and I'm mad at him. We don't talk, Ellie."

"I'll send one of the boys with you," Ellie said.

"You'll not send anybody sneaky enough to get by Will Titus. He has stopped me every single time I come home after dark, no matter how quiet I was."

"One a my men did, the one that brought you in."

"That's because those two camped in the orchard were making noise," Elizabeth said. "Will Titus will make them keep quiet or run them out."

"I can't risk you tippin' him off."

"Ellie, you're making a big mistake."

"Hell, I been makin' 'em all my life. One more or less ain't gonna make much difference."

"You're selling Bart out."

"No. No, I'm not. I'm looking out for me and what's gonna be left o' the gang. Bart ain't got the chance of a snowball in hell. I can't risk my life and the boys for nothin'. Let's have no more yappin' an' that's final."

"Gonna be daylight pretty soon," the man beyond said in a complaining voice.

"Yeah, I know. Ben, you go on down to the blacksmith shop. Go in the back way and get inside the barn somehow. Climb up in the loft and get to that hole in the gable, looking out on the road. If Titus shows up while we're gettin' the boys unchained you know what to do."

"I'm not such a good shot in the dark," Ben said. "Maybe you better send Sam—"

"Sam is with Bart and you damn better do what you're told to do."

"What about me?" Elizabeth asked.

"I'll keep you close to me," Bay said. "I won't let nothin' happen to you. Don't worry."

"Might as well tell the world to stop spinning."

"Go on, Ben. We'll be right along soon as we get Lucian. We gotta use him to cut the boys loose."

The man beside the tree moved closer to the group. Elizabeth recognized Jack Lickey, a man who'd ridden with Bart for as long as any member of the gang.

"Try to talk some sense into Ellie," Elizabeth said.

Lickey shifted his weight from one foot to the other. "She makes sense, Ellie," he argued quietly. "Those three down there chained up ain't worth the trouble. Smart thing to do is haul tail outta here."

"No, I'm not gonna give up," Ellie Bay said stubbornly. "Keep a hand on Elizabeth and don't let her get away. I'm gonna round up Lucian."

After Laney disappeared into the darkness, Cantrell cleared his throat to get attention. "I'm going to visit the Danite camp," he told Grafton and Bowman. "You may want to go with me."

Both of them shook their heads in unison. "I'd just as soon not get into that," Lucian said gravely. "You understand, Bishop?"

Cantrell nodded. "I see no way out of this tangle of circumstance except to let Bart handle it his own way. Though he's certainly not acting like a man in possession of all his faculties."

"He owes a big bill at the store," Grafton said. "I hope he doesn't do anything foolish."

Cantrell gave them all a curt nod and faded into the darkness on what he considered a hopeless mission. The Danites were difficult to talk to let alone deal with.

At the sheep wagon, Bowman and Grafton shuffled uneasily and then silently departed, leaving Lefty and Sam alone.

Sam said, "Where'd Bart go?"

"Probably to visit his daddy's grave," Lefty said, squatting to look inside the sheep wagon. "That bunk don't look too good to me, Sam."

"Well, it look all right to me."

"I'd better go after Bart," Lefty said, rising. "He ought not to be out there all by hisself."

"I'll go with you." Sam rose and stretched.

"No, you stay put. Can't tell what might turn up here."

"All right with me. Whatta y' think's gonna happen, Lefty?"

"Damn if I know," Lefty said irritably. "See you later." He walked away in the direction Bart had taken.

Bart parted the two bottom strands of barbwire enclosing the cemetery and crawled through. The stars had brightened and lent a silvery light to the shadowed area. He passed a new grave and felt a pang in his heart. The Fenton boy. Bart felt responsible for the boy's death in a manner peculiar to his own personal values. He remembered the eagerness of the boy, listening to him avidly, as Bart described the likely route Titus would take into Circle City: "He won't ride directly in, he's a smart one, that fella. He'll cross the Troublesome at the old ford below the bridge, follow that old wagon track west of Little Creek and come out north o' town. He'll be on his toes every step a the way. Just let Bishop Cantrell know, George. That's all you got to do is let the bishop know that Will Titus will be in Circle City come morning."

He'd watched Fenton ride away, never dreaming for a moment that the boy would try out Titus. Afterward, Bart and Brace had rode off to the Dirty Devil, to recover a bank haul cache that had been stashed there against a rainy day.

Laney walked on in a direct line to his father's gravestone. He ran his fingers over the inscription he knew by heart. It was a wide stone, with room for his mother's death date. Her name and date of birth was etched in the stone.

Bart Laney had lived his early youth in awe of his father, a stern, forbidding man who spent much time away from home. "Doing the work of the Lord," his mother always said. He wondered often in those days about his father, why it was that his feeling for him was nearly always tinged with fear. Not that Matthew mistreated him, or Will Titus either, for that matter. It simply was his being so unapproachable, a lofty being who could do no wrong. Not until that day the federal marshals rode in, surrounded the house, and took Matthew Laney prisoner and rode him away in handcuffs for a court trial that ended in his sentence of death, by a firing squad or hanging. Matthew Laney elected to be shot.

A noise in the night brought him out of his reverie. He stepped closer to the headstone and rested his hand on his gun butt.

"Bart, it's me, Lefty."

Laney relaxed. "I'm comin'," he said, walking toward the shadowy shape of Lefty near the fence.

"I want to borrow your gunbelt," Bart said.

"My gunbelt?" Lefty asked in a startled voice. "What in hell for? You know I ain't never loaned my gun—"

"I don't want your gun," Bart said. "Just that left handed holster. And I'll give it back to you soon's I finish with it."

"Ah, god, Bart," Lefty said. "What your sister said about Titus—him shootin' left handed—Bart, you're loco."

"Save all that," Bart said. "Just let me have it."

Lefty slowly unbuckled his belt and slid the holster off it and passed it to Bart. He stuck his gun in his belt and put Bart's holster on his gunbelt and strapped it around his waist. He put his gun back into the holster. "Don't feel right on that side," he complained.

"Won't be for long," Bart said, leaning over to tie the buckskin thong around his left leg. He heard a whisper of sound, heard Lefty grunt and then something hit him a paralyzing blow that drove him toward the ground. He seemed to fall for a long time, and then the dark sky fell in on him.

CHAPTER 18

Will Titus listened to the sound of loud voices and occasional bursts of laughter coming from Remington and Pierpont across the road in the orchard. The noise gave him a strong feeling of being completely isolated and alone. He was irritated, too, that their racket drowned out other sounds that he listened for, and on which his life depended that he hear. He'd debated the wisdom of ordering them out of the orchard to a campsite more distant from his watching and listening post. He had not made up his mind but was leaning toward getting rid of them.

On this night he tried to analyze his feeling, unreasonable, he told himself, of resentment at the camaraderie of the artist and the photographer. It was something he could only guess at because he considered that he'd never had a real friend, not since Bart.

In his life after leaving Circle Valley as a youth, Titus had purposely remained apart from other men. Acquaintances he had and many of them men of power in Arizona, men who cultivated him because one never knew when one would need a favor from a U.S. marshal. He'd shunned those contacts, keeping the men distant without offending them more than he considered necessary. He nevertheless found himself yearning at times for something more than the impersonal relationships he'd established among his peers. I've been formed, he thought, and there's nothing to be done about it.

Growing annoyed with himself, he moved quietly off the porch. He shoved his hat back, expanded his chest, looking up at the glitter of the sky. He detected a faint whisper of a voice on the light wind, a sound that banished his introspection.

Turning back to the porch, he lifted the shotgun and moved quietly across the yard and into the road. He stood there, listening and again picked up the faintest of sounds.

Moving silently, he crossed the road, hearing the murmur of the prisoners and the bursts of laughter from the orchard.

A shape loomed before him as he neared the corner of the barn and he jabbed the twin muzzles forward and into the man's throat. There was a gagging sound that ceased as Titus brought up the butt of the shotgun in a smashing blow to the man's jaw. He whirled then and fired a blast from the shotgun at a shadowy figure a dozen or more feet distant.

Ellie Bay crouching, muttered, "What the hell's goin' on—" He saw one of his own men fire at him from the corner of the barn. Outraged, he screamed, "Goddammit, you're shootin' at me."

Bay, still crouching, pushed Lucian Bowman ahead of him as buckshot struck the anvil and caromed off into the walls of the barn. Bay fired then, and yelled, and another round of gunshots came from behind him. He pushed Lucian forward and then yelled: "Drop!" and flung himself full length on the ground, the whine of bullets overhead. He heard Jack Lickey say something unintelligible, and another shot blasted the night. Bay felt Lucian's body shudder. Leaning forward he saw the blood stain spreading on Lucian's shirt front.

Bay had a fierce desire to get away from there, and a small panic began forming inside him. He fought the panic and scuttled between the smithy and the snubbing post with the cries of the prisoners ringing in his ears. He stopped short as Titus stepped toward him, his pistol glinting in the starlight. Bay triggered his Colt a split second after Titus fired and Bay fell in a crumpled heap and lay still.

Titus went ahead with his pistol at the ready. He bent to take the gun from Bay's hand but it really wasn't necessary.

"You there," Titus said to the prisoners, "keep it quiet."

The chatter of the prisoners stopped at once. Titus walked to the road, and stalked along the edge of the irrigation ditch, in the direction he'd heard another voice. He halted suddenly when a voice came from beyond the massed morning glory. "I got Elizabeth here, Titus, and I'll damn well shoot her if you come another step."

"Elizabeth?" Titus called.

"Yes, Will, he has me all right. Jack Lickey."

"Bay is dead," Titus said. "And Ben might be dead. I hit him a good one with the butt of my shotgun. You're all alone, Jack, and you'd be better off to give your gun to Elizabeth."

"Damn if I will," Lickey said. "There's still Bart, yeah, and Lefty and Sam Agnew—"

"They're not here now," Titus said. "You cut yourself loose tonight, man, and you know it."

It sounded like a sob escaped Lickey. "My horse is down in back of Grafton's store," Lickey said. "I'm goin' there now, and I'm ridin' out, Marshal."

"I'm not stopping you," Titus said, "but you got to let Elizabeth go."

"No, damn it, I got her and I'll keep her for a spell. She's my guarantee you won't try to stop me."

"Kidnaping is serious, kidnaping a woman even more. You take her one step against her will and it's kidnaping."

Lickey laughed and Titus thought he detected a nervous thread in the mirthless cackle. "That's the least o' my worries. Stay right where you are, Marshal, where I can see you." His voice changed, indicating to Titus that he was moving.

Titus stood still, his eyes searching the vine of morning glory for any motion, however small. He had not caught a glimpse of Lickey and he swung a little to listen better, watching the area he'd last heard Lickey's voice. He guessed that Lickey was backing away, holding Elizabeth in front of him, but keeping low so as to be screened by the morning glory vine which grew rampant at that end of the orchard.

He heard a deep sigh come from Lickey as he took a few tentative steps forward without drawing a shot. He reached into his coat pocket and found a shotgun shell. He brought it out and after waiting a period, threw the shell toward the massed vines. It struck with a rustle and drew Lickey's fire, one single shot.

Lickey rose up in view and Titus shot him in the head, aiming across Elizabeth's shoulder. Both Lickey and Elizabeth disappeared from sight.

Titus went forward slowly, his pistol ready. Elizabeth was rising when he reached Lickey and she adjusted her clothing and said in a dull, uncaring voice, "You got him, Will."

Titus leaned over and took away the man's gun. He briefly touched his hand to Lickey's heart and detected no beat. He straightened and touched her arm. "Lucian's been hit. Go fetch Doc McNair."

"I've got to see about Mama," she said and went past him. When she reached the road she turned back. "Doc always comes when he hears shooting." She turned, lifted her skirts and ran toward her house.

Titus went back to Lucian. He found the blacksmith sitting on the ground, his head in his hands.

"Can you walk?"

Lucian dropped his hands. "Yes, Will, I believe I can if you'll give me a hand up."

Titus helped him to his feet and Lucian would have fallen if Titus hadn't caught him. Titus bent and got his shoulder under Lucian and lifted him, walking slowly across the road to Grafton's front porch. He laid the blacksmith out on the porch and straightened up as Jenny Gardner came into the yard.

She stopped abruptly and then gave a little cry and ran to him. "You're shot!" she cried, putting her arms around him, and tugging him toward the porch. "You lay down there and be still while I run for the doctor."

"I'm not shot," Titus said. "That's Lucian's blood you see there." He didn't move, feeling the warmth of her body against his and the softness of her hands.

Ceasing all movement, she stepped away hastily. "Take off

your shirt and I'll scrub it out—no, I'll go get the doctor for Brother Bowman."

"Not needful, here he comes now."

Without taking time to anchor his buggy horse, McNair came swinging toward them with his black bag in his hand. He knelt beside Bowman and began unbuttoning his shirt. He pushed Bowman back as the smith tried to rise. "I'll take a look, Lucian, if you don't mind."

"Go ahead, Doc. Who shot me?"

"It might have been me," Titus said. "I didn't know Bay had you with him."

"He was bringing me to set the prisoners loose. Said he needed three more men for his gang."

"He wouldn't get them there. Not one of them is worth a bucket of horse suds."

"I'll make him a cup of beef broth," Jenny said hurriedly and went into the house.

Bowman winced as McNair probed at a round hole between his ribs. "I got to talk to you, Will."

"Talk away."

"It's about the Massacre," Bowman said painfully. "I was there. I took part in it. I did as much—"

"Lucian, you're not going to die," McNair said gently. "You got a double-ought buckshot between the sixth and seventh ribs and my guess is it touched the bottom of your lung. But you'll be all right in a week or two so don't go making a deathbed confession."

"I got to talk, Doc. There's no other way I can see to do it. Like I said, Will, I did as much killin' as any other man in the company." He groaned and not from the pain of his wound.

Titus heard this in silence. He felt hardly any emotion at hearing Bowman's words and he found this surprising. Bowman was leading up to something more important and so Titus waited for him to go on.

"You have to understand the times. We were a driven people. The Hebrews in Egypt had it easy compared to us. We were harried from pillar to post. The Prophet Brigham selected this desolate country because he thought no one in his right mind would want it and try to take it from us.

"I'm not makin' excuses, Will. I'm simply tryin' to explain how it all come about." He bent a fierce gaze on Titus as though daring him to dispute what he was saying.

Titus nodded. "I'm somewhat familiar with Mormon history, Lucian," he said dryly.

"Maybe you think you do. You can't know full well because you weren't there. But I was there and I know whereof I speak."

"I'm all ears, Lucian."

"Want me to get on with it, hey? Well, all right. We didn't get the peace and tranquillity we wanted. First, there was the gold rush of forty-nine. The fever touched here, yes, more in Salt Lake City than down this way. The ruffians and desperados among the gold rushers headin' for California outnumbered the good people. When all that simmered down, the U. S. Government sent a Gentile mind you, in here to be Territorial Governor. We couldn't accept that, so the government sent troops in to bring us to terms. It was like hell, just one thing after another, year after year after year."

"You're telling me what I've known all my life."

"No, you don't see it or you'd not be so stubborn. I said I wanted to explain, but I must say now that I can't explain. A kind of madness seized us. We remembered too well the Missouri and Illinois mobs, our President Joseph Smith beaten and tarred and feathered, and finally murdered.

"A party of California-bound people come through here 'bout 1857. Gentiles they were, mostly from Arkansas and Missouri. They turned off at Fort Bridger and headed south to make California that way, fearing to get snowed in up in the mountains.

"They made trouble every step of the way. They sold spoiled beef to the Indians, fouled water wherever they stopped, and set the sagebrush afire. They abused every Mor-

mon settler they met, and said and done things that left a
string of enemies behind them. Then, when they began running out of food, and when our people refused to sell to them
they took it by force.

"That's how it all happened, Will, so help me God. A kind of
madness grabbed hold of us when they gave us the worst in-
sult of all, saying that our wives were whores, the mothers of
our children."

"You're getting all worked up and in a lather, Lucian,"
McNair said. "I'm ordering you to stop this. Stop it right now."

Lucian relaxed visibly. "I guess I've said it all."

"That you have, indeed. Come on, I'll help you in my buggy
and drive you home. Which one, Lucian?"

"I'll go to Melinda's," Lucian said. "That's where Brace
spent the night. I've got to counsel that boy on mendin' his
ways."

"You've got to rest, that's what you've got to do," McNair
said briskly. "Come now, give me a hand, Will."

Titus and McNair assisted Lucian to his feet and supported
him to the buggy and helped him in. Titus stepped back as
McNair got into the buggy, took a seat beside Lucian, and
lifted the reins. "Think about what Lucian told you, Will," he
said, and clucked to his horse and moved away.

A moment later Remington rode his horse out of the orchard, leading his pack animal. He guided his mount across
the road and stopped near Titus. "Well, Marshal, I've had my
fill of the wild west. I'm heading back east."

"It's a wise move."

Remington nodded agreement. "I believe I have a future as
an artist. I'd not want to see it end here in this country where
the possibility of stopping a stray bullet seems great."

"Good day to you, Mr. Remington."

Remington put up his hand and turned his horse north.
Titus watched him out of sight. He was turning back to his
rocking chair when he stopped again. The town undertaker
had a team and wagon stopped in front of the smithy and with

the help of an elderly man was loading Ben Timmons' body into the wagon. Pierpont came from the orchard with his tripod over his shoulder. "Hey there, wait just a minute."

Pierpont and the undertaker talked for a few minutes and then the undertaker nodded agreement. While Pierpont stood his tripod on its three legs, the two men lugged the bodies of Lickey and Bay up beside the wagon, and laid out all three men side by side. Pierpont set up his camera and disappeared under the black hood. He emerged in a moment, directing the undertaker in arranging the bodies so the bullet holes and blood would be visible.

Titus stalked across the road. "What the hell do you think you're doing?"

Pierpont stared at him. "Taking pictures, of course. There are people who'll pay to see the bodies of dead criminals, desperate men—"

"I'll give you just one hour to get out of town," Titus said.

"Marshal, you can't—"

"If you're not taking steps in five minutes to move out, I'll shoot your camera full of holes," Titus said deliberately. "After that, I'll burn your wagon and shoot your horses. Now, do you understand what I'm telling you?"

"Marshal, this is my living—"

"Take pictures of the mountains, of the wild life. Better yet, head west to the big water and take pictures of the Pacific Ocean. I hear it's a sight to behold. And better than desecrating the dead."

"Marshal, I'm not—"

"In addition to doing what I've already promised, I'll kick your butt right up around your neck if you don't get moving right this minute. Understand?"

"Yes, sir, Marshal, I'm going." His face burning, Pierpont began dismantling his equipment. In a few minutes he disappeared into the orchard.

Waving the undertaker to get on with his work, Titus retired to his rocker on the porch. He was not particularly elated when in less than a half an hour, Pierpont drove his wagon out of the orchard, into the road, and headed south at a trot. The undertaker had disappeared and nothing moved that Titus could see in the great distances around him. Even the crows had vanished.

Bart Laney regained consciousness to the sounds of firing, intermittent, sharp, vengeful from pistols, following the booming shotgun blasts.

He tried to rise and found he was unable to move. His hands were tied behind his back. His feet were bound together. He looked for Lefty and did not see him. He did see a group of men across the small fire from him. They were looking off into the darkness from where the sound of shooting died away after the short series of firing stopped. Laney heard a groan and realized it came from his own throat. These men all of a mould, tall, thin, dressed in dark clothing, and well-armed, exuded an air of violence held in leash. Their horses were picketed, and ready for riding, their belongings secured behind saddles. It was plain they'd slept in their clothing, and with their weapons handy. The Danites, he automatically tagged them, with a hazy thought. He swung his head. One of the Danites noticed the movement and came to stand over him.

"How you feelin'?"

"How the hell you expect a man to feel who's been hit over the head?"

"I'm sorry for that," the tall man said seriously. "Bishop Cantrell ordered us not to hurt you more than necessary. We doin' this for your own good."

"I don't need it."

"Well, it's been decided. You got nothin' to say about it. Soon's we finish our work you'll be let loose."

"And what's that work?"

"We're wipin' out Gentility. On our way there we'll take care of the demon marshal."

"There's not enough of you for that."

"We'll see."

Two shots sounded in the distance and then nothing. "What's the shooting about?"

The Danite shook his head. "We don't know. Brother Hiram has gone to investigate."

"Where's my man, Lefty?"

Shaking his head sadly, the Danite said, "Brother Parley used too much force. Your friend is dead."

Laney kept his head still for when he moved it he felt a wave of dizziness. His head throbbed as he forced himself to think. His half-formed plan, which had been simply to ride up to Titus and shoot it out if the marshal barred his way to his last visit with his dying mother seemed foolish now.

"What're you waiting for?" Laney asked the Danite leader.

The man looked down at him, his expression a study in self-righteous ferocity. "Bishop Cantrell is movin' his people out of Circle City come daylight," he said in a preaching voice. "When they're removed from danger we'll do our work." His deepset eyes held a fanatical gleam.

Laney was familiar with the fearful reputation of the Danites but this was his first face-to-face encounter with them. "That's mighty thoughtful of you."

"I sense a spirit of levity in your remark."

Laney felt like cursing but restrained himself. He rolled away so he didn't have to look at the man. He listened as Hiram reported to his leader: "Can't make nothin' out of what's goin' on. Whatever happened it all took place around Lucian's blacksmith shop."

"Maybe it won't matter in the long run," the leader said. "Let's repair to the unfinished temple for a prayer vigil. We can also see from there when the people are all gone. It'll be daylight soon."

"What about Brother Laney?"

"I'm not your brother," Laney said but they ignored his words.

"He'll be all right here for the time. Before we attack one of our number will have to come back and stand guard over him. Now, let's be on our way."

Laney watched the group mount and ride silently south. It was eerie the way they moved without making noise. Seldom speaking, and then only in low-voiced monosyllables, these men were normally under control of the President of the Church. The most feared, fanatical, and secret band in the country, their president, John Taylor, was a fugitive from the army of marshals trying to arrest him. Taylor's followers hid him out, passing him from home to home, from town to town. So this band was beholden to no one, only to their own sense of bitter retribution and blood vengeance.

After sounds of their departure faded, Laney rolled toward the fire, which had almost burned itself out. He managed to get close enough to feel the heat on his face. He mentally selected a stick, one end unburned and projecting from the campfire, the other end sending up tiny tendrils of flame. Rolling over, he thrust his bound hands out, feeling for the stick of wood. His fingers closed on it. He slowly inched away from the fire, bringing the stick with him. It was hot to touch but not hot enough to burn. He slowly turned the stick in toward him, thrusting a small rock under it to keep it off the ground and the flame alive. He inched his way toward the flame, feeling the burn of the flaming part of the stick of wood. He put the rawhide thong binding him against the stick and slowly moved his hands upward, positioning them directly over the flame. He felt the bite of fire and smelled the sickening odor of burned flesh. He kept the rawhide pressed against the flaming stick until the agony caused him to draw away. He lifted his hands, his face drenched with sweat, his arms aching with the intensity of forcing himself to undergo the torture.

Dizziness overcame him and he fell into a pit of blackness.

It was bright daylight when he recovered consciousness. The fire had died away. His wrists pained him as he moved slightly, feeling the skin peel away. He could hear the gurgle of the creek and became aware of his intense thirst. The pounding of hooves came to him and one of the Danites, the one called Hiram, rode into the clearing. He got down from his horse and strode to Laney.

"Won't be much longer," he said, and then he noticed what Laney had done. "You tried to get away." He squatted and inspected the piggin string binding Laney's hands together. "You got a mess o' blisters, an' that's about all." Hiram rose and went to his horse and got his canteen. He returned to Laney, knelt and poured water over Laney's wrists. The cooling water felt good for a moment.

"The water'll cause the rawhide to shrink," Laney mumbled.

"I know that. I'm goin' to put another piggin string on you." He got out his knife and cut the charred rawhide which fell away, relieving the pressure on Laney's wrists.

Hiram went to his horse to find another rawhide string, while Laney felt around with his hands, reaching for a stone, anything to use as a club. He found nothing.

The Danite returned with the piggin string and leaned over as Laney drew his knees up to his chest and struck out with all his strength. One boot missed but the heel of the other caught Hiram on the point of his chin and upended him, sending him shoulders first into the ground. He lay there, unmoving.

Laney scrabbled toward Hiram and drew out the man's knife and slashed the rawhide binding his feet together. He got to his feet, staggered, and caught on to Hiram's saddle horn to steady himself. The horse danced away but Laney hung on and let himself be dragged while he talked softly and soothingly to the horse, who slowed and then stopped. Laney snagged the reins on a bush and staggered to the creek where he fell to his hands and knees to drink thirstily and noisily.

When he'd satisfied his thirst he got to his feet, walked back to Hiram and took the man's gun from its holster and shoved it in his own. He caught up the reins, mounted Hiram's horse and splashed across the creek, and headed south, along the western fringes of Circle City.

CHAPTER 19

Driving rigs of all kinds, people moved south on the road in front of Titus. Buckboards, wagons, surries, buggies, even a cart or two, all piled high with personal belongings, and holding women and children streamed past him.

"What's it all mean?" Titus asked Jenny Gardner.

Standing with her hands on her hips, she shook her head. "The brothers tell me nothing. But I suppose Bishop Cantrell is clearing the town."

"For what reason?"

"Expecting trouble, I suppose. You should know all about that." She looked at him resentfully. "I hear the Danites are camped up above the cemetery."

Remembering Cantrell's threat to call in the Danites, Titus agreed with a nod. The last wagon passed. Dust brown and thick hung in the air but began to move as a light wind sprang up from the southwest.

"Look!" Jenny exclaimed.

Titus stopped rocking and followed her pointing finger. He came to his feet with a feeling almost of relief.

Bart Laney rode down the road in the wake of the mass evacuation, looking neither to right nor left.

"Go in the house, Jenny," Titus said tersely. "Or better yet, light out for your own home."

Laney came on, slowly, slack in the saddle, seemingly unconcerned. The horse fretted under a tight rein.

Titus reached for his shotgun. He saw Jenny standing where she had been, unmoving, staring at Laney with a look of dread on her pretty face. Titus touched her arm. "Clear out, Jenny," he said.

Shaking violently, her eyes filled with tears. "You're all such damn fools!" she cried and whirled and ran into the house.

Titus walked to the edge of the road, the shotgun nestled in the crook of his arm. Halting, he waited, putting down the surge of emotion he couldn't identify.

Laney stopped his horse and leaving the reins wrapped around the horn, stepped to the ground. The horse drifted to the side of the road and began grazing.

"I'm goin' in to see my ma," Laney said.

"Give me your gun first."

"No, I'm not gonna do that, Will. I've never handed my gun over to anybody and I'm not gonna start now." His demeanor reminded Titus of a time in their boyhood when they quarreled about dividing chores to be done.

"If we hurry we can get this over with before the Danites get here."

"When did you start shooting with your left hand?"

Bart's face twitched in a way that Titus remembered as a prelude to lying. "I shoot with either hand." He made a movement that placed his feet farther apart and crooked his elbow slightly. "We might as well get this over with."

"I always knew it would come to this. Make your move, Bart, when you're ready."

Low thunder rolled from the north. A band of black-garbed riders surged into view. A rifle cracked from the middle of the riders and it seemed that Grafton's front porch exploded. Wood splinters flew in all directions. Titus' prized telescope landed at his feet, bent and broken. *My saddlebags,* Titus thought, *all my ammunition.*

"Danites!" Bart yelled and wheeled away, trotting toward the blacksmith shop. Titus followed at a lope as a full volley blossomed from the approaching riders. The three prisoners crowding behind the snubbing post tried to position themselves to get the most protection.

Rushing past at a full gallop, the riders poured a withering fire into the smithy, bullets clanging off iron and whining into the walls of the barn. Once past the smithy, they wheeled, raising a cloud of dust, and came charging back down the road. Three of them peeled off and circled, to come on the barn from the rear. Titus picked off one rider with the left barrel of his shotgun. He had no more shotgun ammunition so he laid the weapon aside and drew his .38, and waited for the returning riders.

"I thought the Danites were your friends." Titus aimed at the leading rider and knocked him out of the saddle, slowing the charge but not stopping it.

"When they get the blood lust like this they ain't nobody's friend." Bart fired and hit a horse, which reared, squealing, dumping the rider into the dust. The man scuttled away into the bushes as his horse thrashed wildly about.

Riding hard and shooting, the Danites swooped by. One of the prisoners fell, moaning. Titus felt the burn of a bullet on his shoulder, ignoring it as he fired. As the tail-end rider swept past, Titus reloaded his .38 and saw that Bart was firing his Colt with his right hand. Damn fool, he thought, coming at me left-handed.

Two riders swept around the corner of the barn. Titus shot the lead rider as the horse skidded and Bart toppled the other with one shot. Bart and Titus looked at each other as the Danites regrouped in front of Grafton's store, readying for another run at them.

"Bart?"

"I'm listenin'."

"Arizona Territory is getting a new governor, a man who owes me a big favor. I think I can swing a deal for you that won't be like the other time when they tried to trick you into giving yourself up."

Bart squinted at the Danites. "Wonder what them crazies are up to now?"

"You're not listening."

"Yeah, sure. You gonna get me a pardon and I'll go to work shovelin' manure and live happy ever after."

"There are plenty of jobs once you have an unconditional pardon. Buffalo Bill offered me a job in his Wild West show. He'd jump at a chance to hire you."

"I wouldn't be free anywhere except in Arizona Territory, Will, and you know it."

"I think it could be worked out. What do you say?"

"I heard you lost your job. Old fatboy Flagle fired you. Why don't you pitch in with me. It's a pretty loose life, lots of excitement, yeah, and plenty o' spendin' money." He tilted his head. "With you alongside me I could expand my operation."

"I'm still a marshal 'til I turn in my badge."

A Danite rode out from the group of riders with a white rag fluttering from his rifle barrel.

"Watch 'em," Bart warned as Titus rose and strode out of the blacksmith shop and halted near the snubbing post.

"For God's sake let us loose," Shagrun sobbed. "We all gonna git kilt out in the open like this."

Smoke rose against the wall of the house across the street, where his belongings had been stored. Titus had no time to contemplate his loss as the Danite stopped his horse in the middle of the road in front of him. "Well?"

"We just want to ride on to Gentility," the Danite said. A gaunt man, his deepset eyes blazed with a fanatical light and his silver-spotted beard waved in the wind. "We ain't got no quarrel with Bart. He's done a lot for the brethern."

"You'd be well advised to turn around and go back where you come from. You got nothing but trouble here."

"Gentility's an abomination in the sight of God. It has got to be destroyed."

"The women and children, too?"

"There are no children in Gentility, Marshal. Only harlots, murderers and fornicators."

"That may be true but it's not for you to judge."

"I'm not judging. It's a revelation from Almighty God."

"Danite, turn around. Ride north to Orem. Your prophet is under siege there. He needs your help and without it he's to die."

"You'll die and be damned, too," the Danite muttered and wheeling his horse, loped the animal back to the waiting group.

Titus watched them until a crackling sound reached his ears. He turned. The wall behind the demolished rocking chair where his ammunition had exploded was enveloped in flames licking hungrily at the old wood. Jenny Gardner came out the door with a bucket in her hand. She tilted the bucket, pouring water on the growing blaze.

Titus started forward as the Danites broke into a full gallop and bore down on him. He ran hard to avoid the oncoming riders but an outside horse ran into him, knocking him into the dirt. The bunch rushed past as Titus rolled over and sat up. He was aware that Jenny was kneeling beside him her arms around him. She had a smudge of dirt on her cheek.

Bart came toward them, looking at the Danites disappearing around a turn near the bridge over the Troublesome. He held his pistol loosely in his right hand.

Jenny Gardner grabbed Titus' gun from its holster and holding it with both hands, pointed the gun at Bart. "You're not to touch him," she hissed. "I'll shoot you, Bart, if you so much as raise a hand to him."

Bart stopped, his face frozen. His lips twitched, a minute motion that might have been the start of a smile. "I didn't come over here to hurt him, Jenny Gardner," he said. "We'd better get busy or old man Grafton's house's gonna burn down." He holstered his gun and went on to pick up the bucket Jenny had dropped, and trotted toward the creek.

Titus clambered shakily to his feet. He took his gun from Jenny and shoved it into his holster. "Grafton got another bucket somewhere around?"

"I'll get it." She hurried into the house, past the leaping flames and emerged with a bucket which she gave to Titus. He joined Bart and they trotted back and forth between the creek and the house, gradually putting the fire out.

Titus surveyed the smoking ruins of his belongings. "Every damn thing I owned," he said.

"We start with nothin', we end with nothin'," Bart said.

"I can do without your damn philosophizing."

Bart grinned, seeming boyish. "We had it easy considerin' what Gentility's gonna get when them Danites get there."

Titus tried to brush some of the dirt off his coat. He gave it up. He cleared his throat. "Go on in, Bart, and see ma. She's waited a mighty long time."

"You comin' with me?"

Titus thought about it for a long moment. Across the road, Dr. McNair and the town undertaker moved about their business. He looked down at Jenny. She nodded almost imperceptibly. "I'm coming in with you," Titus said.

CHAPTER 20

Limping on sore feet and a wounded leg, Kid Ringbolt led his equally lamed horse into Circle City just before noon, not knowing the day or the week it was, let alone the month. He bore little resemblance to the carefree, happy youth who'd left Kansas what seemed a century ago. His thin brown beard had grown wildly in all directions and his stringy hair hung well below his ears. Gaunt from near starvation and suffering deep pain from the bullet wound in his leg, he had moments of delirium, when he was a small boy in Texas again, and wondering at how he come to be where he was. Then it would all come back and he'd go on.

That hole in his leg scared him more than anything. It drained odorous pus and the fevered flesh had streaks of red from his knee to his ankle.

Ringbolt halted at the town cemetery. A group of men were digging graves, six of them he counted. The men noticed him leaning on his horse, and stopped working. A tall, slope-shouldered man laid down his shovel and walked to the fence. The other grave diggers stopped all action to watch.

"Strangers ain't welcome in Circle City," the tall man said in a steely voice. "Just keep right on goin' an' don't tarry none."

"I got to see a doctor," Ringbolt said dully. "I got a gunshot in my right leg an' it pains me awful."

"Doctor's house is right down there," the man said, pointing to a frame house. "Soon's he fixes you up be gone with you."

"I come to see Marshal Titus."

"You listen to what I told you. Soon as Dr. McNair fixes you, skedaddle. Circle City can do without the likes o' you."

"What do you know about me?"

"Enough to want you out of our town." The tall man waved him impatiently onward, then wheeled and strode back to the grave diggers and they resumed their work.

Spiritlessly, Ringbolt continued, thinking that Circle City was a mighty unfriendly town. He had to pull as hard as he could on the reins. His pony was ready to lay down and die. "Not much better off than me," Ringbolt muttered. Texas had never been like this.

A man working on a big stone building ignored him. The man had laid out a row of stones and was picking them up and placing them on the waist-high wall, using a trowel to scrape off the excess mortar.

The door to the stone house next to the construction site opened and a beefy-shouldered man with a full beard emerged, straightened his hat, and came toward Ringbolt.

"We're not accommodating strangers," the large man said with authority. "I'm Bishop Cantrell and I command you to make haste and depart at once."

A measure of rationality came to Ringbolt. "I'm hurt, an' my horse is lame. I'm not certain I can keep goin'."

"There's a doctor over there," the bishop said, pointing. "Get what you need and begone before dark sets in."

Ringbolt lapsed into a delirium and babbled senselessly. The bishop turned back into his house. Ringbolt stood there, feeling too sick to move. He wanted to lie down but he knew if he did he'd never get up again. Some inner drive pushed him ahead slowly and he got as close to McNair's house and office as he could. He slumped against his horse, indecisive, looking at the house which was quiet, with no movement around, until a boy rounded the corner and stopped short, staring at him.

"I been shot," Ringbolt said thickly. "Must be infected. Doctoring is what I need."

"Doc's been workin' straight through the last night and day," the boy said, not unfriendly like the others. "He's sleepin' but I'll try to get him up. Tie your horse and go on in the house."

"My pony's in worse shape than me," Ringbolt said, dropping the reins. "He ain't goin' no place nohow." He staggered as he went toward the steps. The boy jumped forward to support him, guiding him up the steps, across the porch and into the combined waiting room and office.

"Gee, you sure stink. I'm Jason Gardner."

"Well, it's my own stink an' the least o' my worries." He sank into a canebottomed chair and leaned back, closing his eyes.

As in a dream he heard voices from upstairs and the clump of boots on wooden steps. He felt a cool hand on his forehead. He opened his eyes to see a haggard-faced man with gray bristles on his face peering down.

"Come on, boy, get on the table in yonder. Here, Jason, give him a hand."

With the help of Jason and the doctor, Ringbolt found himself on a narrow table. He felt the doctor messing around with his boot and he yelled when the boot came off.

"Sorry, boy, it had to come off so's I could get a look at it. Don't look too good. Here, take a sip of this." He raised Ringbolt's head and put a beaker to his lips. Ringbolt sipped and screwed up his face in distaste. "Go on, take it all," the doctor said. "It'll kill some of the pain."

Ringbolt gave up. He let himself go, giving in to the urge to just plain not give a damn. He could hear only a faint murmur. Maybe it's the heavenly angels, he thought, and then even those fragmented sensations went away.

When he awoke he was lying on a bed in an upstairs room. He could see a cottonwood tree through the window and filmy balls blowing away in the wind. In the far distance he could see the mountains shining in the sunlight, capped with puffy clouds.

"Awake, hey?"

He turned his head to look at the awkward boy who'd

helped him into the house. He struggled with his memory, trying to remember the boy's name. "Jason," he said.

Jason grinned. "Remembered, hey? You were just 'bout
done in when you got here."

"Everybody I run into told me to get outta town," Ringbolt
said. "I come all the way from Texas to see Marshal Titus."

"You and about a hundred other people," Jason said. "He's
done gone, nobody knows when he left."

"Well, did he kill or capture Bart Laney?"

"Nobody knows. Bart's gone, too. Hey, maybe I been talkin'
too much."

The doctor came in and walked to stand beside the bed.
"You're a lucky young man. Another day and I couldn't have
saved that leg."

Ringbolt felt a shock go through him. He couldn't imagine
himself as a one-legged man. He wouldn't be able to do anything with just one leg.

"When you took that bullet in your leg, a piece of the boot
went in ahead of the bullet. Otherwise that leg of yours would
never have healed without being removed. You'll be up and
around in a few days."

"In a few days? I've been told to vamoose outta here."

The doctor nodded. "The town's been through what might
amount to a battle. Lots of shooting and so on. The citizens
have had enough and they won't take any more."

"Dunno what I'll do."

"I've made arrangements with Jason here to watch out for
you for a few days, until you're able to travel. The brethern
will suffer you to stay a little longer."

"What happened to Titus and Laney?"

"Better to not ask that question. They're gone and that's
good enough for Circle City." He looked at Jason. "You can
take him down to your place after dark. Keep him there until
he's fit to ride." To Ringbolt, he said: "I've had a look at your
horse. He'll be all right in a few days. Just starved, and needs
shoes all around."

At dusk, Jason helped Ringbolt into McNair's buggy and drove down the road, recounting historic sites: Grafton's store, past the smithy and Grafton's house, and the Laney house across the street; the big fight had taken place right here, Jason solemnly announced.

A few minutes later, Jason guided the team into the yard of a small, neat house. "I brought your horse down yesterday," he said. "Gave him feed and water. Kind of shaggy but that pony is tough an' he'll come back. There is where I live."

"All by yourself?"

"Yep, all by my lonesome."

"Titus and Laney really gone?"

"Yep. Left between two days. That's how Marshal Titus explained it when somebody disappeared durin' the night."

"Did the Marshal and Laney leave together?"

"Nobody knows."

"Damn, I come all the way from Texas to learn about peace officerin' from Titus," Ringbolt complained. "Look, one of the Masterson brothers gave me this Colt." He pulled the gun from his holster and displayed it. "I saved his life."

Jason drew back at the sight of the gun. "The Mastersons? Bat and Ed?"

"Sure. Don't worry 'bout this gun. I run outta shells a long time ago," Ringbolt said, putting the gun away.

"C'mon," Jason said gruffly. "Let's get you inside. Not much left here but the stove and bed. Guess we can get along."

"You're mighty young to be livin' alone."

They were inside the house now, and Jason helped Ringbolt stretch out on the bed. "Yep. I'll be leavin' here myself purt' soon, quick as Bishop Cantrell closes the deal on the house."

"Well, who did you live with?"

"My ma. She's gone now, an' I'm gonna meet her in a month or so. Don't ask so damn many questions, and I'll fry some spuds and eggs."

In the morning, Ringbolt hobbled out to the small corral to

check on his horse. The pony neighed at him as he approached, and Ringbolt said, "Hi to you, too."

Jason came up behind him. "Brother Bowman, he's our blacksmith here, will be puttin' shoes on your horse. Can't ride that pony without shoes."

"Say, that's a mighty fine lookin' horse," Ringbolt said, admiringly, at the tall black gelding staring over the fence.

"He's a fine one, all right," Jason said. "His name is Peso. He belonged to Marshal Titus."

"Say, you sure Titus is alive? A bunch o' men were diggin' a lotta graves when I got in town yesterday."

"Yesterday? Man, you got here three, four days ago. You was outta your mind for a long spell. Doc Mac thought you was gonna lose—"

"Don't say it," begged Ringbolt. "Gives me shivers to even think about it."

"Well, Titus is all right, wherever he is. His stuff got all blowed up when the Danites shot into his saddlebags. They were filled with ammunition."

"Danites? Blowed up?" Ringbolt sounded bewildered. "What in heck is Danites?"

"They're a bunch a fanatics, blood vengeance people. Some call them the Avenging Angels, or Dark Angels, all kind a scary names."

"Mormons?"

"You got it."

"Are you Mormon?"

Jason shook his head. "Nope. What you got against Mormons?"

"Nothin'," Ringbolt said hastily. "Though they do strike me as mighty peculiar at times. If you own the Marshal's horse, how'd he get out a town?"

"First place, I don't own Peso, just keepin' him. Like I said, Marshal's stuff got blowed up, along with his saddle. So he bought a team an' wagon from Bishop Cantrell. He had some prisoners to take back to Tucson. Probably halfway there by now. I'm goin' down myself soon as Bishop Cantrell closes the deal on this house."

"Maybe I could ride along with you."

Jason had looked forward to the long ride with anticipation and at the same time with a certain fear. It was a long ride through some bad country. The thought of company appealed to him. He said, "By golly, that would be great. It beats hell out of travelin' alone."

"Amen," Ringbolt said. "Tucson would be that much closer to Texas."

"You goin' back to Texas?"

"I been thinkin' on it. The more I see of this country the better Texas looks." Then too, there was a lot he'd like to learn about the last days of Marshal Titus in Circle City. He knew Jason would be doing a lot of talking on the long ride south, and he looked forward to it.